A Breath of Life
(Pulsations)

ALSO BY CLARICE LISPECTOR

AVAILABLE FROM NEW DIRECTIONS

Água Viva

The Foreign Legion

The Hour of the Star

Near to the Wild Heart

The Passion According to G. H.

Selected Crônicas

Soulstorm

A BREATH OF LIFE
(Pulsations)

Clarice Lispector

Translated from the Portuguese by Johnny Lorenz

Preface by Pedro Almodóvar & Benjamin Moser

Edited by Benjamin Moser

A NEW DIRECTIONS BOOK

Originally published as *Um sopro de vida: pulsações*. Published by arrangement with
the Heirs of Clarice Lispector and Agencia Literaria Carmen Balcells, Barcelona.

New Directions gratefully acknowledges the support of
MINISTÉRIO DA CULTURA
Fundação BIBLIOTECA NACIONAL

First published by New Directions as NDP1222 in 2012
Manufactured in the United States of America
New Directions Books are printed on acid-free paper
Design by Erik Rieselbach

Library of Congress Cataloging-in-Publication Data
Lispector, Clarice.
[Sopro de vida. English]
A breath of life (pulsations) / by Clarice Lispector ; translated by Johnny
Lorenz ; edited by Benjamin Moser ; with a preface by Pedro Almodóvar and
Benjamin Moser.
p. cm.
ISBN 978-0-8112-1962-4 (acid-free paper)
I. Lorenz, Johnny. II. Moser, Benjamin. III. Title.
PQ9697.L585S613 2012
869.3'42—dc23   2012006506

10 9 8 7 6 5 4

New Directions Books are published for James Laughlin
by New Directions Publishing Corporation
80 Eighth Avenue. New York 10011

Contents

Benjamin Moser & Pedro Almodóvar: An Exchange on "A Breath of Life"

Les Eyzies-de-Tayac-Sireuil
November 11, 2011

Dear Mr. Almodóvar,

Caetano Veloso has written to you about our project to translate Clarice Lispector into English and I would very much like for you to consider contributing an introduction.

When I saw *The Skin I Live In* I was struck by the similarities between the film and Clarice's theme in this posthumous book, which has never before appeared in English. The title, *A Breath of Life*, refers to the creation, mystical or "Frankensteinian," of one being by another. When I saw it I thought: Pedro Almodóvar will love Clarice. And Caetano thought the same.

Like Caetano, who discovered her at age 17, when he still lived in a small city in the interior of Bahia, I fell for Clarice when I was young, in a college Portuguese course in the United States. Ever since, I dreamed of making her better known outside Brazil.

Two years ago, I finally published a biography of Clarice

Lispector, *Why This World*. Now, with these translations, we are taking the next step.

The biggest question that occurs to me as I read *A Breath of Life* is: Was Clarice, more or less dying as she wrote it, mad? Because at many points it reminds me of the diaries of Vaslav Nijinsky, which you surely know: a journey into madness.

But there is also, hidden within this book, a terrible story that I discovered when I was researching my biography. It was known that Clarice was born to Jewish parents in the Ukraine in 1920, and that the Lispectors had arrived as refugees in Brazil when she was still an infant.

What was not known, because of the shame that still predominates in many Jewish families, is that, in that period of war, starvation, and racial persecution, her mother had been raped in a pogrom by Russian soldiers, and that she had consequentially contracted syphilis, which was then incurable.

According to the folk superstitions of the remote area where they lived, a woman with syphilis could be cured by pregnancy. And so that is what her parents did.

The result of this attempt to save her mother was Clarice Lispector herself. For her mother, however, the pregnancy cured nothing. And Clarice, for the first nine years of her life, was forced to watch her mother agonizing, paralyzed, exiled, dying.

Feeling the guilt of having failed in her attempt to cure her mother, the girl started telling stories in which an angel, a saint, a god, came to cure her. These stories failed.

The tragedy is the origin of one of the twentieth century's greatest writers. And until the very end of her life—until *A Breath of Life*—she never lost the hope of repairing the world through mystic means.

In this book she creates Angela because, as she says, she needs someone to save. But at the end of the book she knows that she has to let her die. And the little girl's dream returns, literally, in the last pages she wrote.

Last night I had a dream within a dream. I dreamed that I was calmly watching actors working on a stage. And through a door that was not locked men came in with machine guns and killed all the actors. I began to cry: I didn't want them to be dead. So the actors got up off the ground and said: we aren't dead in real life, just as actors, the massacre was part of the show. Then I dreamed such a good dream: I dreamed this: in life we are actors in an absurd play written by an absurd God. We are all participants in this theater: in truth we never shall die when death happens. We only die as actors. Could that be eternity?

But here, too, she cannot let Angela die. She knows, as she says, that if Angela dies, so too will she. Instead of killing her, she imagines herself as a film director and lets her fade off into the distance.

She was telling these stories until her own death. During her last journey to the hospital where she would die, she said: "Let's pretend that we're not going to the hospital, that I'm not sick, and that we're going to Paris."

So [her best friend recalled] we started making plans and talking about everything we would do in Paris. The taxi driver, poor thing, already tired from working all night long, timidly asked: "Can I go on the trip too?" And Clarice said: "Of course you can, and you can even bring your girlfriend." He said: "My girlfriend is an old lady, seventy years old, and

I don't have any money." Clarice answered: "She's coming too. Let's pretend you won the lottery." When we got to the hospital, Clarice asked how much it was. Only twenty cruzeiros, and she gave him two hundred.

Needless to say, she never went to Paris: she died six weeks later.

I have followed your career since *Women on the Verge of a Nervous Breakdown* (I was twelve, I saw it in the "art" cinema in Houston, my hometown). And I've seen every movie since.

The people I love, in my experience, always end up loving one another. At least I hope that you too will fall for Clarice, even in this unfinished and hieratic book. In fact I have no doubt: it's almost impossible for you not to.

If that's the case, a word from you would help the great Clarice reach many more people. This is the most important project of translation into English of a Latin American author since the complete works of Jorge Luis Borges were published a decade ago.

Excuse this long letter: but I get excited when I talk about her.

Yours sincerely,
Benjamin Moser

Dear Benjamin,

As my assistant told you, I can't write a prologue for *A Breath of Life*, the stupendous and highly original novel by Clarice Lispector, and not because I don't like it: to the contrary. I have never written a prologue to a book, though I have often been asked to. Sometimes because the book didn't interest me and sometimes because the book interested me too much, as is the case with *A Breath of Life*.

I have so much respect for great literature and, especially with books that excite me, I always feel I am not up the task, that a few words of mine wouldn't help the book be better understood. I think a prologue ought to add something new to the work it precedes and I never feel I have anything to add. In this case I also simply lack the time.

This is a thrilling book to read, but it's very difficult to write about it. Without wanting to compare my work to Lispector's,

I have heard on more than one occasion comments similar to your own about my last film from certain critics who liked it and didn't want to revert the same old topics.

Speaking of *Breath* and *Skin*, I found a paragraph that defines transgenesis in an exquisite and precise way. "I want the colorful, confused and mysterious mixture of nature. All the plants and algae, bacteria, invertebrates, fish, amphibians, reptiles, birds, mammals concluding man with his secrets." I can't think of a more beautiful definition of transgenesis, though Lispector was thinking of something quite different. We are already publishing the screenplay of *The Skin I Live In*, and I'm going to suggest placing that quote at the beginning of the book.

The novel is full of memorable phrases about literary creation ("Writing is without warning") and the passing of time ("you don't start at the beginning, you start in the middle, you begin with the instant today"), the desperation and the multiplicity of the individual ("I live losing sight of myself. I need patience because I am many paths, including the fatal dead-end alley"), including the need to speak to oneself, the search for an interlocutor and finding it inside oneself ("the woman I invented because I needed a facsimile of dialogue").

This book has a similar effect on me as the first novels I read by J. M. Coetzee. Each phrase accumulates such a quantity of meanings; it is so dense, rotund, and rich that I halt before it as before a wall. I like it very much but am not qualified to accompany a text of such magnitude. I think a writer would have to do it.

Many thanks for thinking of me. I hope we meet some day.

Best wishes,
Pedro Almodóvar

Introduction

FOR CLARICE LISPECTOR, MY FRIEND, *A BREATH OF LIFE*
would be her definitive book.

Begun in 1974 and finished in 1977, on the eve of her death,
this book, so difficult for her to produce, was, in the words of
Clarice, "written in agony," for it was born from a painful impulse she was unable to contain. During this same period she
was also writing *The Hour of the Star*, her last published novel.

For eight years I lived with Clarice Lispector, participating
in her creative process. I wrote down her thoughts, typed her
manuscripts and most of all shared in her moments of inspiration. As a result, she and her son Paulo entrusted me with the
organization of the pages of *A Breath of Life*.

And so it was done.

OLGA BORELLI

And the LORD God formed man of the dust of the ground, and breathed into his nostrils the breath of life; and man became a living soul.

—Genesis 2:7

The absurd joy par excellence is creation.

—Nietzsche

The dream is a mountain that thought must climb. There is no dream without thought. To play is to teach ideas.
—Andréa Azulay, 10 years old

There will be a year in which there will be a month, in which there will be a week in which there will be a day in which there will be an hour in which there will be a minute in which there will be a second and in that second will be the sacred not-time of death transfigured.
—Clarice Lispector

A Breath of Life
(Pulsations)

"I want to write pure movement."

THIS IS NOT A LAMENT, IT'S THE CRY OF A BIRD OF PREY. An iridescent and restless bird. The kiss upon the dead face.

I write as if to save somebody's life. Probably my own. Life is a kind of madness that death makes. Long live the dead because we live in them.

Suddenly things no longer need to make sense. I'm satisfied with being. Are you? Certainly you are. The meaninglessness of things makes me smile complacently. Everything surely must go on being what it is.

Today is a day of nothing. Today is down to the wire. Could there be a number that is nothing? that is less than zero? that begins where there is no beginning because it always was? and was before always? I tap into this vital absence and I'm a young man again, both contained and complete. Round without beginning or end, I am the point before the zero, before the period of the sentence. From zero to infinity I walk without stopping. But at the same time everything is so fleeting. I always was and just as quickly was no longer. The day runs along aimlessly outside and there are abysses of silence within me.

The shadow of my soul is my body. My body is the shadow of my soul. This book is my shadow. Excuse me, may I pass by? I feel guilty when I don't obey you. I am happy at the wrong moment. Unhappy when everyone's dancing. I've heard that cripples rejoice just as I've heard that the blind can be glad. Because unhappy people make up for it somehow.

Life has never been as current as it is today: a hair's breadth from the future. Time for me means the dissolution of matter. The rotting of the organic as if time were a worm robbing the fruit of its pulp. Time does not exist. What we call time is the movement of the evolution of things, but time itself does not exist. Or it exists immutably and into time we transfer ourselves. Time passes too quickly and life is so short. And so — to avoid being swallowed by the voracity of the hours and the news that makes time rush by — I cultivate a certain tedium. That's how I savor every loathsome minute. And I cultivate too the empty silence of the eternity of our species. I want to live many minutes within a single minute. I want to multiply myself to take in even the desert regions that give the idea of eternal immobility. In eternity time does not exist. Night and day are opposites because they are both time and time cannot be divided. From now on, time will always be the current moment. Today is today. I'm stunned and at the same time suspicious that I've been given so much. And tomorrow I shall once again have a today. There is something painful and pungent about living the today. The paroxysm of the highest and sharpest note of an insistent violin. But then there's habit and habit numbs. The stinger of the bee in the flowering day that is today. Thank God, I have enough to eat. Our daily bread.

I wanted to write a book. But where are the words? all the meanings have been exhausted. Like the deaf and the mute we communicate with our hands. I wanted permission to write the scraps of words while accompanied by a rustic harp. And to dispense with being discursive. Like this: pollution.

Do I write or not?

To know when to quit. Whether to give up—this is often the question facing the gambler. No one is taught the art of walking away. And the anguish of deciding if I should keep playing is hardly unusual. Will I be able to quit honorably? or am I the type who waits stubbornly for something to happen? something like, for instance, the end of the world? or whatever it might be, maybe my own sudden death, in which case my decision to give up would be beside the point.

I don't want to race against myself. A fact. What becomes a fact? Should I be interested in the event itself? Have I been reduced to filling these pages with information about "facts"? Should I make up a story or do I allow my chaotic inspiration free rein? There's so much false inspiration. And when real inspiration arrives and I don't realize it? Would it be too horrible to want to move closer to the lucid self within? Yes, and it's when the self no longer exists, no longer makes demands, that it joins the tree of life—and that's what I struggle to attain. To forget oneself and yet to live so intensely.

I'm afraid to write. It's so dangerous. Anyone who's tried, knows. The danger of stirring up hidden things—and the world is not on the surface, it's hidden in its roots submerged in the depths of the sea. In order to write I must place myself in the void. In this void is where I exist intuitively. But it's a terribly dangerous void: it's where I wring out blood. I'm a writer who fears the snares of words: the words I say hide others—which? maybe I'll say them. Writing is a stone cast down a deep well.

A light and gentle meditation on the nothing. I write almost completely free of my body. As if levitating. My spirit is empty because of so much happiness. I'm feeling an intimate freedom comparable only to riding a horse through the fields without any destination. I'm free of destiny. Perhaps my destiny is to reach freedom? there's no wrinkle on my soul spreading out in delicate froth. No longer am I being assailed. And it's delightful.

I'm hearing music. Debussy uses the froth of the sea dying on the sands, ebbing and flowing. Bach is a mathematician. Mozart is the impersonal divine. Chopin reveals his most intimate life. Schoenberg, through his self, reaches the classical self of everyone. Beethoven is the stormy human elixir searching for divinity and only finding it in death. As for me, I've got nothing to do with music, I only arrive at the threshold of a new word. Without the courage to expose it. My vocabulary is sad and sometimes Wagnerian-polyphonic-paranoid. I write very simple and very naked. That's why it wounds. I'm a gray and blue landscape. I rise in a dry fountain and in the cold light.

I want to write squalidly and structurally as though with the acute angles of a rigid, enigmatic triangle plotted with ruler and compass.

Does "writing" exist in and of itself? No. It is merely the reflection of a thing that questions. I work with the unexpected. I write the way I do without knowing how and why — it's the fate of my voice. The timbre of my voice is me. Writing is a query. It's this: ?

Could I be betraying myself? Could I be altering the course of a river? I must trust that abundant river. Or maybe I'm damming a river? I try to open the flood-gates, I want to watch the water gushing out. I want every sentence of this book to be a climax.

I must be patient for the fruits will be surprising.

This is a quiet book. And it speaks, it speaks softly.

This is a fresh book—recently emerged from nothingness. It is played delicately and confidently on the piano and every note is clean and perfect, each distinct from the others. This book is a carrier pigeon. I write for nothing and for no one. Anyone who reads me does so at his own risk. I don't make literature: I simply live in the passing of time. The act of writing is the inevitable result of my being alive. I lost sight of myself so long ago that I'm hesitant to try to find myself. I'm afraid to begin. Existing sometimes gives me heart palpitations. I'm so afraid to be me. I'm so dangerous. They gave me a name and alienated me from myself.

I feel as though I'm still not writing. I foresee and want a way of speaking that's more fanciful, more precise, with more rapture, making spirals in the air.

Each new book is a journey. But a journey with eyes covered thro' seas never before discovered—the muzzle on the eyes, the terror of the dark is total. When I feel an inspiration, I die of fear because I know that once again I'll be traveling alone in a world that repels me. But my characters are not to blame and I treat them as best I can. They arrive from nowhere. They are inspiration. Inspiration is not madness. It's God. My problem is the fear of going mad. I have to control myself. There are laws that govern communication. Impersonality is one condition. Separativity and ignorance are sin in a general sense. And madness is the temptation to be totally power. My limitations are the raw material to be worked as long as I don't reach my objective.

I live in the living flesh, that's why I make such an effort to give thick skin to my characters. But I can't stand it and make them cry for no reason.

Self-moving roots that are not planted or the root of a tooth? For I too cast off my chains: I kill what disturbs me and good and evil disturb me and I head definitively to encounter a world that is inside me, I who write to free myself from the difficult burden of a person being himself.

In every word a heart beats. Writing is that search for the intimate truth of life. Life that disturbs me and leaves my own trembling heart suffering the incalculable pain that seems necessary for my maturity—maturity? I've lived this long without it!

Yes. But it seems the time has come to fully accept the mysterious life of those who one day shall die. I must begin by accepting myself and not feeling the punitive horror of every time I fall, for when I fall the human race inside me falls too. To accept myself fully? that is a violation of my very life. Every change, every new project is scary: my heart is scared. And that is why each word of mine has a heart where blood flows.

Everything I'm writing here is forged in my silence and in shadows. I see little, I hear almost nothing. I finally dive into myself down to the birthplace of the spirit that inhabits me. My source is obscure. I'm writing because I don't know what to do with myself. I mean: I don't know what to do with my spirit. The body tells a lot. But I don't know the laws of the spirit: it wanders. My thought, with the enunciation of the words mentally blossoming, without my saying or writing anything afterwards—this thought of mine in words is preceded by an instantaneous vision, without words, of the thought—the word that follows, almost immediately—a spatial difference of less than a millimeter. Before thinking, then, I've already thought. I suppose that the composer of a symphony only has the "thought before the thought," is what can be seen in this very quick mute idea little more than an atmosphere? No. It's actually an atmosphere that, already colored with the symbol, lets me sense the air of the atmosphere from which everything comes. The pre-thought is in black and white. The thought with words has other colors. The pre-thought is the pre-instant. The pre-thought is the immediate past of the instant. Thinking is the concretization, materialization of what was pre-thought. Really pre-thinking is what guides us, since it's intimately linked to my mute unconsciousness. The pre-thought is not rational. It's almost virginal.

Sometimes the feeling of pre-thinking is agonizing: it's the tortuous creation that thrashes in the shadows and is only freed after thinking—with words.

You demand from me a tremendous effort of writing; please, I beg your pardon, my dear, allow me to pass by. I am a serious and honest man and if I don't tell the truth it's because the truth is forbidden. I don't put what's forbidden to use but I free it. Things obey the vital breath. We are born to enjoy. And enjoying is already being born. When we were fetuses we enjoyed the total comfort of the maternal womb. As for me, I know nothing. What I have enters me through my skin and makes me act sensually. I want the truth which is only given to me though its opposite, through its untruth. And I can't stand everyday life. That must be why I write. My life is one single day. And that's how the past for me is present and future. All in a single dizziness. And the sweetness is such that it causes an unbearable itch in the soul. Living is magical and wholly inexplicable. I understand death better. Being everyday is an addiction. What am I? I'm a thought. Do I have the breath within me? do I? but who does? who speaks for me? do I have a body and a spirit? am I an I? "That's exactly right, you are an I," the world answers me terribly. And I am horrified. God must never be thought because either He flees or I do. God must be ignored and felt. Then He acts. I wonder: why does God demand our love? possible answer: so that we might love ourselves and in loving ourselves, forgive ourselves. And how we need forgiveness. Because life itself already comes muddled with error.

The result of all this is that I'll have to create a character— more or less as novelists do, and through this character understand. Because I cannot do it alone: solitude, the same that exists in every one, makes me invent. And is there another way to be saved? besides creating one's own realities? I have the strength for this like anybody else—isn't it true that we ended up creating a fragile and mad reality that is civilization? this civilization guided only by dreams. Every invention of mine sounds to me like a layman's prayer—such is the intensity of feeling, I write to learn. I chose myself and my character— Angela Pralini—so that perhaps through us I might understand that lack of definition of life. Life has no adjective. It's a mixture in a strange crucible but that allows me in the end, to breathe. And sometimes to pant. And sometimes to gasp. Yes. But sometimes there is also the deep breath that finds the cold delicateness of my spirit, bound to my body for now.

I wanted to initiate an experiment and not just be the victim of an experiment I never authorized, that merely happened. That's why I'm inventing a character. I also want to shatter, not just the enigma of the character, the enigma of things.

This I suppose will be a book made apparently out of shards of a book. But in fact it is about portraying quick flashes of mine and quick flashes of my character Angela. I could grab onto every flash and go on about it page after page. But it so happens that the essence of the thing is often in the flash. Each entry in my diary and in the diary I made Angela write, scares me a little. Each entry is written in the present. The instant is already made of fragments. I don't want to give a false future to each flash of an instant. Everything happens exactly at the moment in which it's being written or read. This passage here was actually written in relation to its basic form after I reread the book because as the book progressed I didn't have a clear understanding as to which way to go. Yet, without giving greater logical explanations, I clung entirely to the fragmentary aspect in Angela as in myself.

My life is made of fragments and that's how it is with Angela. My own life has an actual plot. It would be the history of the bark of a tree and not of the tree. A bunch of facts that only the senses would explain. I see that, without meaning to, what I write and what Angela writes are passages that might be called random, though within a context of ...

That's how the book occurs to me this time. And, since I respect what comes from me to myself, that's exactly how I write.

What is written here, mine or Angela's, are the remains of a demolition of soul, they are lateral cuts of a reality that constantly escapes me. These fragments of book mean that I work in ruins.

I know that this book isn't easy, but it's easy only for those who believe in the mystery. As I write it I do not know myself, I forget myself. The I who appears in this book is not I. It is not autobiographical, you all know nothing of me. I never have told you and never shall tell you who I am. I am all of yourselves. I took from this book only what I wanted—I left out my story and Angela's. What matters to me are the snapshots of sensations—sensations that are thought and not the immobile pose of those waiting for me to say, "say cheese!" Because I'm no street photographer.

I've already read this book through to the end and I'm adding to this beginning something for you to keep in mind. It's that the end, which shouldn't be read beforehand, comes back to the beginning in a circle, a snake swallowing its own tail. And, having read the book, I cut much more than half of it, I only left what provokes and inspires me for life: a star lit at dusk.

Do not read what I write as a reader would do. Unless this reader works, he too, on the soliloquies of the irrational dark.

If this book ever comes out, may the profane recoil from it. Since writing is something sacred where no infidel can enter. I am making a really bad book on purpose in order to drive off the profane who want to "like." But a small group will see that this "liking" is superficial and will enter inside what I am truly writing, which is neither "bad" nor "good."

Inspiration is like a mysterious scent of amber. I have a small piece of amber with me. The scent makes me sister to the sacred orgies of King Solomon and the Queen of Sheba. Blessed be your loves. Could it be that I am afraid to take the step of dying at this very instant? Careful not to die. Yet I am already in the future. This future of mine that shall be for you the past of someone dead. When you have finished this book cry a hallelujah for me. When you close the last page of this frustrated and dauntless and playful book of life then forget me. May God bless you then and this book ends well. That I might at last find respite. May peace be upon us, upon you, and upon me. Am I falling into discourse? may the temple's faithful forgive me: I write and that way rid myself of me and then at last I can rest.

The Daydream Is What Reality Is

ANGELA

THE LAST WORD WILL BE THE FOURTH DIMENSION.
Length: her speaking
Width: beyond thought
Depth: my speaking of her, of facts and feelings and of her
beyond-thought.

I must be legible almost in the dark.

I HAD A VIVID AND INEXPLICABLE DREAM: I DREAMED
I was playing with my reflection. But my reflection wasn't in a
mirror, but reflected somebody else who wasn't me.

Was it because of this dream that I invented Angela as my
reflection? Everything is real but moves lei-sure-ly in slow motion. Or it jumps from one theme to another, disconnected. If I
uproot myself I expose my roots to wind and rain. Brittle. And
not like blue granite and the stone of Iansã without cracks or
fissures. Angela for now has a swathe of fabric over her face
that hides her identity.

As she speaks she begins removing this swathe—until her
face is naked. Her face speaks unpolished and expressive. Before unmasking her I shall cleanse the air with rain and prepare
the soil for plowing.

I will avoid sinking into the whirlpool of her river of liquid
gold glimmering with emeralds. Her mud is reddish. Angela
is a statue that cries out and flutters around the canopy of the
trees. Her world is only as unreal as the life of anyone who
happens to read me. I raise high the lantern so she can glimpse

the road that is a wrong turn. Stupefied and with uninhibited joy I watch her rise with a ruffling of wings.

To create her I must plow the land. Is there some breakdown in the computer system of my ship while it crosses spaces in search of a woman? a computer made of pure silicon, with the equivalent of thousands of microscopic transistors fixed to its polished and gleaming surface with the noonday sun beating down in a mirror, Angela is a mirror.

I want her to be the means by which the highest axioms of mathematics are solved within a fraction of a second. I want to calculate through her the answer to seven times the square root of 15 to the third power. (The exact figure is 406.663325.)

Angela's brain is embedded in a protective layer of plastic that makes it practically indestructible—after I die Angela will keep vibrating. A statue always being relocated by the crazed disturbing buzz of three thousand golden bees. An angel carried by blue butterflies? An angel isn't born and doesn't die. An angel is a spiritual state. I sculpted her with twisted roots. It's only out of impudence that Angela exists in me. As for me I reduce everything to a tumult of words.

We are all sentenced to death. While I write I might die. One day I shall die amidst random facts.

—It was God who invented me and gave His breath to me and I became a living being. And so it is that I present to myself a person. And therefore I think that I am sufficiently born to try to express myself even if with rough words. It's my interior that speaks and sometimes without connection to my conscious mind. I speak as though someone were speaking for me. Perhaps the reader speaks for me?

I do not remember my previous life, since I have the result which is today. But I remember tomorrow.

How shall I begin?

I'm so frightened that the way to enter this writing has to be suddenly, without warning. Writing is without warning. So I start with the instant like someone throwing himself into suicide: the instant is all of a sudden. And so it is that I've all of a sudden arrived in the middle of a celebration. I'm flustered and apprehensive: it's not easy to deal with Angela, the woman I invented because I needed a facsimile of dialogue. An accursed celebration? No, the celebration of a man who wishes to share with you, Angela, something that absorbs me completely.

Angela Pralini is the celebration of birth. I don't know what to expect from her: will I just have to transcribe her? I must be patient so as not to lose myself within me: I live losing sight of myself. I need patience because I am many paths, including the fatal dead-end alley. I am a man who chose the great silence. Creating a being who stands in opposition to me is within the silence. A spiraling clarinet. A dark cello. But I manage to see, however dimly, Angela standing beside me. Here she is coming a little closer. Then she sits by my side, rests her face in her hands and weeps for having been created. I console her making her understand that I too feel the vast and shapeless melancholy of having been created. I'd rather have stayed in the immanescence of the sacred Nothing. But there is a wisdom of nature that caused me, after being created, to move about even though I didn't know what my legs were for. Angela, I too made my home in a strange nest and I too obey the obstinacy of life. My life wants me to be a writer and so I write. It's not by choice: it's an intimate command.

And just as I received the breath of life that made me a man, I breathe into you who become a soul. I introduce you to myself, visualizing you in snapshots that already happen in the midst of your inauguration: you don't start at the beginning, you start in the middle, you begin with the instant today.

The day begins. The day is a crusher of paving-stones for the street that I hear in my room. I wanted in my way of nailing you down for myself for nothing to have modifications or definitions: everything would move in a circular motion.

Sometimes I feel that Angela is electronic. Is she a high-precision machine or a test-tube baby? Is she made of screws and springs? Or is she the living half of me? Angela is more than I myself. Angela doesn't know she's a character. Besides I too might be the character of myself. Could it be Angela feels that she's a character? Because, as for me, I sometimes feel that I am someone's character. It's uncomfortable being two: me for me and me for others. I live in my hermitage which I only leave to exist in myself: Angela Pralini. Angela is my necessity. But I still don't know why Angela lives in a kind of constant prayer. A pagan prayer. Ever-new excommunicated terrors. She's achieved a native language.

Angela doesn't know herself, and she has no clear image of herself. There is a disconnection in her. She confuses in herself the "for-me" with the "from-me"! If she weren't so dumbstruck and paralyzed by her own existence, she would also see herself from the outside in—and would discover that she is a voracious person: she eats with an intemperance bordering on complete greed as if bread were being taken from her very mouth. But she believes she's merely dainty.

I'm sculpting Angela with stones from the hillsides, until I shape her into a statue. Then I breathe into her and she becomes animated and surpasses me.

You must not forget that I am basically different from Angela. Aside from everything else, the man I am, he tries anxiously in vain to follow the byzantine meanderings of a woman, with attics and corners and angles and living flesh—and suddenly spontaneous as a flower. I as a writer cast seeds. Angela Pralini was born of an ancient seed that I cast upon the hard soil millennia ago. To arrive at me were millennia upon the earth necessary?

How far do I go and where do I already start to be Angela? Are we fruit of the same tree? No—Angela is everything I wanted to be and never was. What is she? she's the waves of the sea. While I'm the dense and gloomy forest. I'm in the depths. Angela scatters in sparkling fragments. Angela is my vertigo. Angela is my reverberation, being an emanation of mine, she is I. I, the author: the unknown. It's by mere coincidence that I am I. Angela seems like something intimate that became exteriorized. Angela is not a "character." She's the evolution of a feeling. She's an idea incarnated in the being. In the beginning there was only the idea. Then the word came into contact with the idea. And then the word was no longer mine: it transcended me, it was everyone's, it was Angela's.

I've always wanted to find someday a person who would live for me because life is so full of useless things that I can only bear it through extreme muscular asthenia, I suffer from moral indolence in living. I tried to make Angela live in my place—but she too wants only the climax of life.

Maybe I created Angela in order to have a dialogue with myself? I invented Angela because I need to invent myself—Angela is a startled woman.

All I know I cannot prove. What I imagine is real, or else on what basis could I imagine Angela, who roars, bellows, moans, pants, bleating and growling and grunting.

I feel as though I've already secretly achieved what I wanted and I still don't know what I achieved. Could that be the somewhat dubious and elusive thing vaguely called "experience"?

AUTHOR: I fear when the earth was formed. What a tremendous cosmic boom.

Through layer upon subterranean layer I reach the first man created. I reach the past of others. I recall this infinite and impersonal past which is without intelligence: it's organic and it's what worries me. I didn't begin with myself when I was born. I began when the slow dinosaurs had begun. Or better yet: nothing begins. It's like this: only when man takes notice through his simple gaze does a beginning appear to him. Yet—I give the appearance of contradiction—I already began many times. I'm beginning right now. As for Angela, she was born with me now, she strains to exist. Except I'm marginalized despite having a wife and kids—marginalized because I write. For instead of following the already-opened road I took a detour. Detours are dangerous. Whereas Angela is compliant and social.

Angela has within her water and desert, populace and hermitage, abundance and neediness, fear and defiance. She has within her eloquence and absurd muteness, surprise and antiquity, refinement and crudeness. She's baroque.

I extract my feelings and words from my absolute night.

The difference between me and Angela can be felt. I cloistered in my narrow, anguished little world, not knowing how to leave to breathe in the beauty of what's outside me. Angela, agile, graceful, full of the ringing of bells. I, seemingly bound to a destiny. Angela with the lightness of someone who has no end.

Angela is continually being made and has no obligations to her own life or to literature or any art, she's purposeless.

Angela consoles herself for existing by thinking: "I at least have the advantage of being me, and not some random stranger."

I tame Angela. I have to cross mountains and desolate areas, flattened by cyclonic storms, inundated by torrential rains and scorched by a high and voracious sun as merciless as ideal justice. I traverse this woman like a ghost train, across hills and valleys, through sleeping cities. My hope is to find the slightest hint of an answer. I advance with caution.

—I know that in Montserrat—mountains of intimate comfort and pure solitude—some ceramic objects were found from the Stone Age and the Bronze Age, and the skeletons of two Iberians, the people who primitively inhabited the region. This awakens an excited soul that flickers within me at the mercy of unfettered winds. I wish I could make Angela aware of it but I don't know how to fit into her life this knowledge that implies an exit from oneself into the terrain that is clear and of pure information. Precious information that situates me millennia ago and fascinates me with the dryness of the communication of the phrase.

Cold and stupefying.

I imagined the clear sound of drops of water falling into water—except that this minimal, delicate noise would be amplified beyond sound, in enormous crystalline drops with a wet ringing of bells sinking. In the cold and stupefying air the statues asleep.

I am writing by groping along.

Could it be I really know that I am I? This question arises because I notice that Angela doesn't seem to know herself. She doesn't realize that there is a center inside her and that it's hard as a nut. From which words radiate. Phosphorescent.

Dejection. The taste of a crushed cigarette.

Sensation is the soul of the world. Is intelligence a sensation? In Angela it is.

I recognize that my imitators are better than I am. Imitation is more refined than raw authenticity. I am under the impression that I've been imitating myself a bit. The worst plagiarism is plagiarizing yourself. The struggle is hard: if I am weak I shall die. As for Angela, I must say that I know perfectly well that she's only a character. I'm absolutely lucid and can speak with some objectivity. But what I don't understand is why I invented Angela Pralini. It was to deceive someone. Perhaps. The little popularity I have displeases me. And then there are my imitators. But what about me? What style should I turn to if I've already been so used and handled by some people who had the bad taste of being me? I'll write a book so closed that it will only allow passage to a few. Or perhaps I'll never write again. I know nothing. The future—as Angela would say—weighs down on me by the ton. I'm lost on this Sunday that's neither hot nor cold, having already taken refuge in a movie theater.

Could my fatal darkness be the promise of an also-fatal light? It so happens that I fear the fatal light and already have a certain intimacy with the dark.

I've left the territory of the human and therefore left Angela too. I transcended myself with a certain degree of muteness and deafness: I'm living by a thread.

I wished

AUTHOR: I am the author of a woman I invented and to whom I gave the name Angela Pralini. I got along well with her. But she started to disturb me and I saw that once again I'd have to take on the role of writer in order to put Angela into words because only then can I communicate with her.

I write one book and Angela writes another: I've removed the superfluous from both.

I write at midnight because I am dark. Angela writes by day because she is almost always happy light.

This is a book of non-memoirs. It is happening right now, it doesn't matter when this right now was or is or shall be. It's a book like sleeping deep and dreaming intensely—but there's an instant when you awaken, sleep fades away, and only a taste of dream remains in the mouth and in the body, only the certainty of having slept and dreamt remains. I do everything possible to write by chance. I want the phrase to happen. I don't know how to express myself in words. What I feel is not translatable. I express myself better through silence. Expressing myself through words is a challenge. But I'm not up to the challenge. Poor words emerge. And what is the secret word? I don't know and why do I dare? Do I not know just because I don't dare say it?

I am well aware that I am in the dark and feed myself with my own vital darkness. Is my darkness a larva that has inside it perhaps a butterfly? It's so dark that I've gone blind. I simply can't write anymore. I'll let Angela talk for a few days. As for me I think …

ANGELA: Living leaves me atremble.

AUTHOR: For me too life makes me shiver.

ANGELA: I feel anxious and afflicted.

AUTHOR: I see that Angela doesn't quite know how to start. Being born is difficult. Should I advise her to talk more easily about facts? I'm going to teach her to start in the middle. She must stop being so hesitant because otherwise this whole book will be atremble, a drop of water dangling about to fall and when it falls it divides in splinters of scattered droplets. Take courage, Angela, start without paying too much attention.

ANGELA: … and I ask myself whether I'm about to die. Because I write almost in a death rattle and feel dilacerated as in a final farewell.

AUTHOR: Is this ultimately a dialogue or a double diary? I only know one thing: at this moment I'm writing: "at this moment" is a rare thing because only sometimes do I step with both feet on the land of the present: usually one foot slides toward the past, the other slides toward the future. And I end up with nothing.

Angela is my attempt to be two. Unfortunately, however, because of the way things are, we resemble one another and she too writes because the only thing I know anything about is the act of writing. (Though I don't write: I speak.)

I did a quick inventory of my possessions and reached the frightening conclusion that the only thing we have that hasn't been taken from us yet: our own names. Angela Pralini, a name as gratuitous as yours and which became the title of my trembling identity. Where will this identity lead me? What do I do with myself? Since not a single act symbolizes me.

ANGELA: Astronomy leads me to a star of God.

It rises in pure incense that shatters in words of glass.

AUTHOR: My not-I is magnificent and surpasses me. Yet she is I to me.

ANGELA: I was born amalgamated with the solitude of this exact moment and which is so drawn out, and so deep, that it is no longer my solitude but the Solitude of God. I finally reached the moment in which nothing exists. Not even tenderness from me to myself: this solitude is of the desert. The wind for company. Ah but what a dark cold it brings. I cover myself with soft melancholy, and gently rock back and forth, back and forth, back and forth. Like that. Yes! Just like that.

AUTHOR: Angela's words are anti-words: they come from an abstract place inside her where one doesn't think, that dark and vague and dripping place like a primitive cave. Angela, unlike me, rarely reasons: she just believes.

Now because I'm afraid to write, I let you speak, even inconsequentially as I made you. Here you are, in your crazy unintelligible dialogue with me:

ANGELA: I, frightened gazelle and yellow butterfly. I'm no more than a comma in life. I who am a colon. Thou, thou art my exclamation. I breathe myself thee.

I am oblique like the flight of birds. Intimidated, without strength, without hope, without warning, without news—I tremble—I tremble—all over. I cast a sidelong glance at myself.

What an effort I make to be myself. I struggle against a tide in a boat with just enough room for my two feet in a perilous and fragile balance.

Living is an act I did not premeditate. I blossomed from the dark. I am only valid for myself. I must live little by little, it's no good living everything at once. In someone's arms I die completely. I am transformed into energy that has within it the nuclear atomic. I'm the result of having heard a warm voice long ago and having stepped off the train almost before it stopped—haste is the enemy of perfection and that's how I ran toward the city missing immediately the station and the train's next departure and its exceptional moment that awakens such a painful fright which is the whistle of the train, which is farewell.

AUTHOR: Here she is talking as though with me but she talks to the air and not even to herself and only I can take advantage of what she says because she is from me and to me.

Angela is my most brittle character. If she even manages to be a character: it's one more example of life beyond-writing like life-beyond-death and beyond-word.

Do I love Angela, because she says what I don't have the courage to say because I am afraid of myself? or because I think speaking is useless? Because what you speak is lost like breath that leaves the mouth when you speak and that bit of breath is lost forever.

ANGELA: I love you as much as if I were always bidding you farewell. When I'm too alone, I fasten rattles to my ankles and wrists. That way almost all my thoughts are externalized and return to me as replies. My slightest energy makes them vibrate immediately in a quiver of light and sound. I have to be my friend or else I can't bear the solitude. When I am alone I try not to think because I am afraid of suddenly thinking a thing too new for myself. To speak out loud alone and to "what" is to address the world, it's to create a powerful voice that achieves—achieves what? The answer: it achieves the "what." "What" is the sacred sanctity of the universe.

AUTHOR: Neither do I know how to not-think. It happens without effort. It's only hard when I try to obtain that silent darkness. When I'm distracted, I fall into shadow and into the hollow and into the sweet and into the smooth nothing-of-me. I refresh myself. And I believe. I believe in magic, then. I know how to create within me an atmosphere of the miraculous. I concentrate without any object in mind—and I feel myself taken by a light. It's a gratuitous miracle, without form and without meaning—like the air that I inhale deeply until I get dizzy for a few seconds. A miracle is the crux of living. When I think, I ruin everything. That's why I avoid thinking: all I really do is go on going on. And without questions about why or whither. If I think, a thing doesn't turn up, I don't happen. A thing that certainly is free to go as long as it's not imprisoned by thought.

ANGELA: I take deep pleasure in prayer—and making intimate and intense contact with the mysterious life of God. There is nothing in the world that can substitute the joy of prayer.

Today I swept the terrace where I keep my plants. How good it is to handle the things of this world: the dry leaves, the pollen of things (dust is the daughter of things). My daily life is very adorned.

I'm being profoundly happy.

AUTHOR: Speak, Angela, speak even without making sense, speak so that I won't completely die.

ANGELA: I'm in agony: I want the colorful, confused and mysterious mixture of nature. All the plants and algae, bacteria, invertebrates, fish, amphibians, reptiles, birds, mammals concluding man with his secrets.

AUTHOR: I'm going on holiday from myself and letting Angela do the talking. If one day I should read these things I'm writing, I want to find in the black pit of night thousands of mute fireworks but accompanied by the splinters of thousands of singing crystals. That is the dark night I want to find one day outside me and within. Angela has just made me suddenly feel something within and I felt happy. Extremely happy, I don't know why. Do I accept it? No, for some secret reason I feel a great burden of uneasiness and anxiety when I reach the snowy peak of a happiness-light. The too-purified air hurts my body.

Angela has wings.

ANGELA: I really like things I don't understand: when I read a thing I don't understand I feel a sweet and abysmal vertigo.

AUTHOR: When I was a person, and not yet this rigorous being filled with words, I was more misunderstood by me. But I accepted myself as a whole. But the word slowly kept demystifying me and forcing me not to lie. I can still sometimes lie to others. But as for me my innocence ended and I am dealing more with an obscure reality that I nearly, nearly grasp. It's a secret truth, sealed, and I sometimes get lost in its fleeting aspect. I am only worthwhile as a discovery.

ANGELA: I'm an actress to myself. I pretend that I am a particular person but in reality I am nothing.

AUTHOR: I thought that a seven-pointed polyhedron could be divided into seven equal parts within a circle. But I don't fit. I am outside. Is it my fault if I don't have access to myself?

ANGELA: I don't fall into the foolishness of being sincere.

AUTHOR: Anyway, Angela, what is it that you do?

ANGELA: I take care of life.
   The great night of the world when there was no life.

AUTHOR: Angela represents the only person she is: there only exists one Angela. Not a single act of mine is I. Angela shall be the act that represents me.
   I lost sight of my destiny. My asking is never exhausted. I ask. What do I ask for? This: the possibility of eternally asking. I have no mission: I live because I was born. And I shall die without death symbolizing me. Outside of me I am Angela. Inside of me I am anonymous. Living demands such audacity. I feel as lost as if sleeping in the desert of the Treasury Department.

—Angela, now I am speaking directly to you and ask you for the love of God to cry already. Do, please, give your consent and cry. Because, as for me, I can't stand waiting any longer. Scream out in pain! A red scream! And the tears burst the flood-gates and wash a tired face. Wash as if they were morning dew.

ANGELA: Am I pure?

AUTHOR: Purity would be as violent as the color white. Angela is the color of hazelnut.

I have a great need to live from much poverty of spirit and not have any luxury of soul. Angela is luxury and upsets me. I will move away from her and enter a monastery, which is to say, become poor. I chose today to wear some very old trousers and a torn shirt. I feel good dressed in rags, I am nostalgic for poverty. I ate only fruit and eggs, I refused the rich blood of meat, I wanted to eat only what's born without agony, just blossoming naked like the egg, like the grape.

I didn't sleep with my wife last night because a woman is luxury and extravagance, and makes me into two, and I want to be only one in order not to be a number divisible by any other. I drank water while fasting. And slowly entered my own and immeasurable and infinite desert. When in this desert my penury becomes intolerable—I create Angela as a mirage, illusion of optics and spirit, but I must abstain from Angela because she is a richness of soul.

Just now I wanted to make Angela paint.

ANGELA: I'm painting a picture with the name "Meaningless." They are random things—objects and beings without any connection, like a butterfly and a sewing machine.

I'LL RUN THROUGH THE FACTS AS QUICKLY AS POS-
sible because I'm in a hurry. The most secret of meditations
awaits me.

To write I begin by stripping myself of words. I prefer the
poor words left over.

I'll give a quick biographical sketch of Angela Pralini: quickly
because facts and particulars bore me. So let's see: born in Rio
de Janeiro, 34 years old, five foot six and of good family though
the daughter of poor parents. Married an industrialist, etc.

ANGELA: I am as individual as a passport. I've got a police
record. Should I be proud to be part of the world or does it
discredit me?

AUTHOR: There's something sweet in Angela's eyes, something
reckless, a humid velvet, dull pearls but brown and sometimes

hard like two chestnuts. Sometimes she has eyes like those of a cow being milked. Sweaty eyes. A glittering and mellifluous bee that hovers above me in search of my honey to hide it away as it was hidden in me. Angela is still a closed cocoon, as if I were not yet born, until I open myself in metamorphosis, Angela will be mine. When I am strong enough to be alone and mute— then I will free forever the butterfly from its cocoon. And even if it lives for only a day, that butterfly, it is already useful to me: may it flutter its bright colors above the green brightness of the plants in a garden on a summer's morning. When the morning is still early, it looks just like a light butterfly. Whatever is even lighter than a butterfly. A butterfly is a petal that flies.

ANGELA: The dancing of the guests.

Ireland, never shalt thou see me. Malta, of Malta, thou art the prison. A bloody finger points upward. And I remember the future.

Dutch—is what I am. And I am September too. So many fruits the lady has. The dog searching for its own tail. Help! fire! And I am chamber music.

AUTHOR: Angela is a curve in an interminable sinuous spiral. I am upright, I write triangularly and pyramidally. But whatever is inside the pyramid—the untouchable, dangerous and inviolable secret—is Angela. What Angela writes can be read aloud: her words are voluptuous and give physical pleasure. I am geometric, Angela is a spiral, all finesse. She is intuitive, I am logical. She is not afraid to err in the use of words. And I do not err. I am well aware that she is the succulent grape and I am the raisin. I am balanced and sensible. She is free of balance which for her is unnecessary. I am controlled, she doesn't repress herself—I suffer more than she does because I am imprisoned in a narrow cage of forced mental hygiene. I suffer more because I don't say why I suffer.

ANGELA: And I am no more than a promise.
But I am a star. I feel that I am a star. Shattered. I am a shard of glass on the ground.

AUTHOR: This woman is scathing toward herself she is the sharp points of a star. Those sparkling points wound me too. You don't know how to live based on an instant-climax: you feel it but can't prolong it into a permanent feeling. You don't learn from others, you don't learn from yourself. I respect you though you're not my equal. And am I my equal? I am I? This question arises from my observation that you don't seem to know yourself. You might not know that there is a center of yourself and that it's hard as a nut from which your phosphorescent words radiate.

ANGELA: Seriously: what am I?
No answer.
So I throw my body away. Am I Strauss or just Beethoven? Do I laugh or cry? I am name. That's the answer. It's not much.
Suddenly I saw myself and saw the world. And I understood: the world is always someone else's. Never mine. I am the pariah of the rich. The poor in soul keep nothing stored away. The dizziness you feel when in a sudden flash of lightning you suddenly see the brightness of not understanding. I DO NOT UNDERSTAND! For fear of madness, I renounced the truth. My ideas are invented. I don't take responsibility for them. The funniest thing is that I never learned how to live. I don't know anything. All I know is how to go on living. Like my dog. I'm

afraid of the excellent and the superlative. When something starts getting really good I either mistrust it or step back. If I stepped forward I'd be focused on the yellowness of the splendor that nearly blinds.

AUTHOR: Angela is the vibrating tremor of a tense harp-string after it's been plucked: she stays in the air still saying, saying—until the vibration dies spreading out in froth across the sands. Afterwards—silence and stars. I know Angela's body by heart. I just didn't understand what she wants. But I gave her such shape to my life that she seems more real to me than I do.

ANGELA: My life is a great disaster. It's a cruel divergence, it's an empty house. But there's a dog inside barking. As for me—all that's left for me is to bark at God. I'm going back to myself. That is where I find a dead destitute girl. But one night I'll go to the government archives and set fire to everything and all the identity cards of the destitute. And only then do I become so autonomous that I shall only stop writing after I die. But it's no use, the blue lake of eternity doesn't catch fire. I am the one who would incinerate myself down to my bones. I shall become number and dust. Let it be. Amen. But I protest. I protest in vain like a dog in the eternity of the government archives.

AUTHOR: Angela is a lot like my opposite. To have inside me the opposite of what I am is in essence indispensable: I won't give up my struggle and my indecision and the failure—for I'm a great failure—failure serves as the foundation of my existence. If I were a winner? I'd die of boredom. "Getting" isn't my strong point. I nourish myself with what's left over of me and it's very little. There is left over however a certain secret silence.

ANGELA: I only use reason as an anesthetic. But for life I'm a perennial promise of understanding my submerged world. Now that there are computers for almost every type of search for intellectual solutions—I therefore turn back to my rich interior nothing. And I scream: I feel, I suffer, I am happy, I am moved. Only my enigma interests me. More than anything, I search for myself in my great void.

I try to keep myself isolated from the agony of depending on others, and that agony that seems to them a game of life and death masks another reality, a truth so extraordinary that they would keel over in fright were they to face it, as in a scandal. Meanwhile, they're studying, working, loving, growing up, struggling, feeling happy, feeling sad. Life with a capital letter can give me nothing because I'm going to confess that I too must have turned down a dead-end alley just like the others. For I notice in myself, not a pile of facts, and instead strive almost tragically to be. It's a question of survival like eating human flesh when there's no other food. I struggle not against people who buy and sell apartments and cars and try to get married and have children but I struggle with extreme anxiety for a novelty of spirit. Whenever I feel almost a little illuminated I see that I am having a novelty of spirit.

My life is a distorted reflection just as the reflection of a face is distorted in an undulating and unstable lake. Trembling imprecision. Like what happens to water when you dip your hand in it. I'm the faintest reflection of erudition. My receptivity is tuned ceaselessly registering other people's conceptions, reflecting in my mirror the subtle shades of distinctions between the things of life. I who am the result of the true miracle of the instincts. I am a swampy terrain. In me is born a wet moss covering slippery rocks. A swamp with its suffocating intolerably sweet miasmas. A bubbling swamp.

AUTHOR: Trying to possess Angela is like trying desperately to grab hold of the reflection in the mirror of a rose. Yet all I had to do was turn away from the mirror and I would have the rose itself. But then there enters a chilly fear of owning the strange and delicate reality of a flower.

ANGELA: As a practically permanent contact with logic a feeling arose in me that I had never felt before: the fear of living, the fear of breathing. I must struggle urgently because this fear ties me down more than the fear of death, it is a crime against myself. I long for my previous atmosphere of adventure and my stimulating restlessness. I think I still haven't fallen into the monotony of living. I recently started suddenly sighing, deep and prolonged sighs.

AUTHOR: Angela has an invisible diadem atop her thick hairdo. Sparkling drops of musical notes run down her hair.

ANGELA: I am extremely tactile. Great aspirations are dangerous, great risk is inherent to great aspirations. Here is a moment of extravagant beauty: I drink it liquid from the shells of my hands and almost all of it runs sparkling through my fingers: but beauty is like that, it is a fraction of a second, quickness of a flash and then immediately it escapes.

AUTHOR: Since Angela Pralini is a bit unbalanced I would advise her to avoid the dangerous situations that might break our fragility. I say nothing to Angela because it's no use asking her to avoid recklessness since she was born to be exposed and go through every kind of experience. Angela suffers a lot but is redeemed in pain. It's like giving birth: one must pass through the sieve of pain in order to be relieved afterwards seeing before one a new child in the world.

ANGELA: But something broke in me and left me with a nerve split in two. In the beginning the extremities linked to the cut hurt me so badly that I paled in pain and perplexity. However the split places gradually scarred over. Until coldly, I no longer hurt. I changed, without planning to. I used to look at you from my inside outward and from the inside of you, which because of love, I could guess. After the scarring I started to look at you from the outside in. And also to see myself from the outside in: I had transformed myself into a heap of facts and actions whose only root was in the domain of logic. At first I couldn't associate me with myself. Where am I? I wondered. And the one who answered was a stranger who told me coldly and categorically: you are yourself. Slowly, as I stopped looking for myself I ended up distracted and without purpose. I'm good at theorizing. I, who empirically live. I dialogue with myself: I expose and wonder what was exposed, I expose and refute, I pose questions to an invisible audience and they spur me on with their replies. When I look at myself from the outside in I am the bark of a tree and not the tree. I didn't feel pleasure. After I recovered my contact with myself I impregnated myself and the result was the agitated birth of a pleasure completely different from what they call pleasure.

AUTHOR: She experiences the different phases of a fact or a thought but in the deepest part of her she is extrasituational and even deeper and more unreachably she exists without words and is only an unsayable, incommunicable, inexorable atmosphere. Free of scientific and philosophical rubbish.

ANGELA: I like staircases.

AUTHOR: What charms me about Angela Pralini is her elusiveness.

ANGELA: The hard wooden rose that I am. But to purify me there is the pungent myosotis urgently but delicately called "forget-me-not."

AUTHOR: I created Angela, but now it's up to me to create a new man, as Robinson Crusoe created his solitude on this earth that is always strange.

ANGELA: As for me, I offer my face to the wind. I look like I'm bearing news. Joking is one of the most serious things in the world. And I who imagined making music just for fun.

AUTHOR: Traveling through this book while keeping Angela company is tricky like going on a journey with the pure yolk of an egg cupped in the palm of my hand without making it lose its invisible but real surrounding—invisible, but there's a skin made of almost nothing encircling the delicate yolk and maintaining it without breaking so it can keep being a round yolk.
Angela is a yolk, but with a small black droplet in its yellow sun. That means: problem. Besides the problem we have with living Angela adds another: that of compulsive writing. She thinks that to stop writing is to stop living. I control her as much as I can, deleting her merely foolish comments. For

example: she's dying to write about menstruation just to get it off her chest, and I won't let her.

ANGELA: I have such a tendency to be happy. These last few days I've felt radiant and ecstatic about being alive.

AUTHOR: Angela, you're a frightened thing in an ever-new world. This very instant will never be repeated until the end of the centuries.

ANGELA: I'm a privileged being because I'm unique in the world. I all coiled up with I.
   Dodecaphonic music extracts the I. Ah I can't go on. I who dance so crazy. Whoever wants me should be the same way.
   Bells chime, Orpheus sings. I don't understand myself and it's good. Do you understand me? No, you're crazy and don't understand me.
   Bells, bells, bells.

AUTHOR: Angela is someone who steals away from the big city.

ANGELA: I felt the pulsing of the vein in my neck, I felt the pulse and the heartbeat and suddenly recognized that I had a body. For the first time from the matter arose the soul. It was the first time that I was one. One and grateful. I possessed myself. The spirit possessed the body, the body throbbed with spirit. As if outside myself, I looked at me and saw me. I was a happy woman. So rich that I no longer even needed to live. I was living for free.

AUTHOR: Angela lives in an atmosphere of the miraculous. No, there's no reason to be shocked: the miracle exists: the miracle is a sensation. Sensation of what? of a miracle. A miracle is a disposition like the sunflower slowly turning its abundant corolla toward the sun. The miracle is the final simplicity of existence. The miracle is the splendid sunflower exploding from its stem, corolla and roots—and being just a seed. A seed that contains the future.

ANGELA: I went around sowing.

Between the word and the thought my being exists. My thought is pure impalpable insaisissable air. My word is made of earth. My heart is life. My electronic energy is magic of divine origin. My symbol is love. My hatred is atomic energy.

Everything I just said is worthless, no more than foam.

Anguished.

Hungry and cold and humiliated.

Barefoot I greet you: this is my humility and this nakedness of feet is my daring.

I don't want to be only myself. I also want to be what I am not.

AUTHOR: Is Angela my edge? or am I the edge of Angela? Is Angela my mistake? Is Angela my variation?

ANGELA: I like myself a little because I'm astringent. And emollient. And sucupira. And dizzy. Crackling. Not to mention rather estrogenic. I threw the stick at the cat-cat-cat but the cat-cat-cat ... My God, I'm unhappy. Farewell, Day, it's already dusk. I'm Sunday's child.

AUTHOR: Angela is a passion.

ANGELA: I get along better with myself when I'm unhappy: a coming together takes place. When I'm happy, I feel like somebody else. Albeit another version of the same. Someone strangely joyful, whistling, slightly unhappy is more peaceful.

I want so badly to be commonplace and a little vulgar and say: hope is the last to die.

AUTHOR: I'd like to be able to "cure" her of herself. But her— "sickness"? is stronger than my powers, her sickness is the form her life takes.

ANGELA: I am the contemporary of tomorrow.

When I'm alone for a long time, I suddenly don't recognize myself and I frighten myself and get chills all over.

From now on I want more than understanding: I want superunderstanding, I humbly beg that this gift be given me. I want to understand understanding itself. I want to reach the most intimate secret of whatever exists. I'm in full communion with the world.

AUTHOR: Angela lives for the future. It's as if I didn't read today's papers because there'll be newer news tomorrow. She doesn't live off memories. She, like a lot of people, including me, is busy making the present moment slide toward the future moment. She was fifteen when she started to understand hope.

ANGELA: I see the lamp that is lit. My interior is a mess. But I light myself up.

AUTHOR: She's a girl who, while she doesn't seem to disrupt the existence of the thought of the present, belongs more to the future. For her each day has the future of the tomorrow. Each moment of the day is futurized to the next moment in nuances, gradations, a gradual increase of subtle characteristics of sensibility. Sometimes she loses heart, she gets discouraged when faced with the constant mutability of life. She coexists with time.

ANGELA: My ideal would be to paint a picture of a picture.

I am so upset that I never perfected what I invented in painting. Or at least I've never heard of this way of painting: it consists of taking a wooden canvas—Scotch pine is best—and paying attention to its veins. Suddenly, then a wave of creativity comes out of the subconscious and you go along with the veins following them a bit—but maintaining your liberty. I once did a painting that turned out like this: a robust horse with a long and extensive blond mane amidst the stalactites of a grotto. It's a generic way of painting. And, moreover, you don't need to know how to paint: anybody, as long as you're not too inhibited, can follow this technique of freedom. And all mortals have a subconscious. Ah, my God, I have hope postponed. The future is a past that has not yet come to pass.

Do you ever suddenly find it strange to be yourself?

I'm not a dreamer. I only daydream to attain reality.

AUTHOR: She, who is full of lost opportunities.

Her true countenance is so secret. The almost weightlessness of a spider's web. Everything inside her is organized around an enigma intangible in its most intimate nucleus.

ANGELA: My enormous waste of myself. Even so I'm glutted and would like to dump even more my treasures hidden in the ark.

Where's my current of energy? My sense of discovery: even if it took an obscure form. I've always expected something new of myself, I was a shiver of expectation: something was always coming from me or from outside of me.

The thing is I'm endemic.

I can't stand a particular feeling for long because it leads to anguish and my mind becomes occupied with that feeling and I untangle myself from it however I can to regain my freedom of spirit. I am free to feel. I want to be free to reason. I aspire to a fusion of body and soul.

I can't manage to understand on behalf of others. Only in the disorder of my feelings do I understand for myself and what I feel is so incomprehensible that I keep quiet and meditate on the nothing.

AUTHOR: The difference between a liberated imagination and a libertine imagination—the difference between intimacy and promiscuity. I (who have as a job to earn money the profession of judge: innocent or guilty?) try to neutralize the habit of judging because I can't stand the divine role of deciding. I free Angela, I don't judge her—I let her be.

ANGELA: I just entered myself and frightened already want to leave. I discover that I am beyond voracity. I'm an impulse split down the middle.

But once in awhile I go to an impersonal hotel, alone, with nothing to do, to be naked and without function. Is thinking having a function?

When I truly think I empty myself.

Alone in the hotel room, I eat the food with brutish and uncouth satisfaction. For a moment it is true satisfaction—then it quickly settles in.

And so I go to my castle. I go to my precious solitude. To retire. I'm all disjointed. But I already start to notice a shine in the air. A sorcery. My room is a smile. In it there are stained-glass windows. The colors are cathedral-red, emerald-green, sun-yellow and deep blue. And my room is that of a sensual monk.

Here there are evening gales. And sometimes the windows bang—as in ghost stories.

I'm waiting for rain. When it rains I want it to fall on me, copiously. I'll open the window of my room and receive naked the water of the sky.

Gardens and gardens interspersed with musical chords. A bloody iridescence. I see my face through the rain. The stridulating clamor of the piercing wind that sweeps the house as if it were hollow of furniture and people. It's raining. I feel the good summer shower. I have a hut too—sometimes I won't stay in the palace, I'll plunge into my hut. Smelling the forest. And enjoying the solitude.

The proof that I'm recovering my mental health, is that I get more permissive with every minute: I allow myself more freedom and more experiences. And I accept what happens by chance. I'm anxious for what I have yet to try. Greater psychic space. I'm happily crazier. And my ignorance grows. The difference between the insane and the not-insane person is that the latter doesn't say or do the things he thinks. Will the police come for me? Come for me because I exist? prison is payment for living your life: a beautiful word, organic, unruly, pleonastic, spermic, durabilic.

Ah, now I know what I am: I am a scribbler. Help me! fire! fire. Writing can drive a person mad. You must lead a serene life, well appointed, middle class. If you don't the madness comes. It's dangerous. You must shut your mouth and say nothing about what you know and what you know is so much, and is so glorious. I know, for example, God. And I receive messages from me to myself.

I know how to create silence. It's like this: I turn on the radio really loud—then suddenly turn it off. And that's how I capture silence. Stellar silence. The silence of the mute moon. It stops everything: I created silence. In silence you can hear noises more. Amidst the hammer blows I was hearing the silence.

I'm afraid of my freedom. My freedom is red! I want them to put me away. Oh enough with disappointments, I'm so beat up, the back of my neck hurts, my mouth, my ankles, I was flogged on my kidneys—what do I want my body for? what purpose does it serve? just to get beat up? A smack in the face that is swollen and ruddy. I take refuge in roses, in words. Little consolation. I'm inflated. I'm worth nothing.

I was interrupted by the silence of the night. The spacious silence interrupts me, leaves my body in a bundle of intense and mute attention. I'm on the lookout for nothing. Silence isn't the void, it's the completeness.

I read what I'd written and thought once again: from what violent chasms is my most intimate intimacy nourished, why does it deny itself so much and flee to the domain of ideas? I feel within me a subterranean violence, a violence that only comes to the surface during the act of writing.

AUTHOR: I don't write like Angela. Not just because I lack the ability but because I'm more sober, I don't spill myself scandalously. And I only rarely use adjectives.

Angela is a stray dog crossing the deserts of the streets. Angela, a noble mutt, follows the trail of her owner, who is I. But she often meanders away and heads off freely wandering toward nowhere. I leave her in this nowhere, since that's what she badly wants. And if she finds hell in life she herself will be responsible for it all. If she wants to follow me then go ahead because that way I'll be in charge and in control. But it's no use ordering her around: that frivolous creature who loves diamonds and pearls escapes me as the unspeakable emphasis of a dream escapes. Hard to describe Angela: she's just a mood, she's just a way of being, a revealing expression of the mouth but revealing of what? of something I didn't know in her and which now, with no possible description, I barely know, that's all. She breathes to me in whispers what she is and, if I can't hear her because of my own lack of acuity, I'll lose her completely.

If Angela is a potential suicide, as I ended up realizing, do I make her commit suicide? No. I don't have the courage: her life is very precious to me. It's just that she has a taste for danger and so do I.

ANGELA: I faint for no reason.

The last time it only took a second. I fall happily into bed and there's the void, and then just afterward I was saying to myself: it was nothing, it's already over. Hello! Hello! Picasso! Come see me, as a special favor. I'm a plucked chick.

But what fireworks! Commemorating what? I wonder.

I look at myself from the outside in and see: nothing. My dog's worried. There's something in the air. A transmission of thoughts. Why don't people look at me when they speak? They always look at someone else. I resent it. But God looks me right in the pupils of my eyes. And I face him. He is my father-mother-mother-father. And I am they. I think I'll see God very soon. It will be The Encounter. For I take risks.

AUTHOR: Angela stirs my fauna and disturbs me. Does her destiny depend on me? Or was she already pretty much freed from my breath to the point of continuing herself? When I think that I could make her die, I tremble all over.

ANGELA: I ask questions out of nervousness. Dismayed. And ankles? are they very important?

I hear no reply to my question. May God protect my ankles. And the back of my neck. They are essential places in me.

Writing never worked out for me. Others are intellectuals and I can hardly pronounce my lovely name: Angela Pralini. An Angela Pralini? the unhappy one, the one who already suffered so much. I'm like a foreigner in any part of the world. I am from the never.

When I was small I twirled, twirled and twirled around until I got dizzy and fell. I didn't like falling but the dizziness was delicious.

I was addicted to getting dizzy. As an adult I twirl but when I get dizzy I take advantage of that brief moment to fly.

I think that madness is perfection. It's like perceiving. Seeing is the pure madness of the body. Lethargy. A tremulous sensibility making everything around more sensitive and making visible, with a small and impalpable fright. Sometimes a balanced imbalance happens like a seesaw that goes up then drops down. And the imbalance of the seesaw is exactly its balance.

AUTHOR: Angela is organic. She's not stagnant. And she's my impasse. Beyond her I can barely see, beyond her begins whatever I don't know how to say.

ANGELA: Today I woke up feeling such nostalgia for happiness. My whole life I've never been free. I always persecuted myself within me. I became intolerable to myself. I live in a dilacerating duality. I have an apparent freedom but I am imprisoned inside me. I wanted an Olympian freedom. But that freedom is only granted to immaterial beings. As long as I have a body it will submit me to its demands. I see freedom as a form of beauty and that beauty is what I lack.

Author: She is unaware that she's self-sufficient up to a point. So she depends on someone who's got arrhythmia and never obtains the complete dependence that would be the surrender of herself, the abandonment of her soul.

Angela: My roots are in the earth and from it I arise naked.
    Cascade—waterfall.
    I want a great heroic panel—upon which I literally spread-my-self-out. I need grandeur and the smell of grass. I emerge from my abysses with hands filled with cold emeralds, transparent topazes and orchidaceous sapphires.
    I am a vibrant and crystalline burst of clarinet.

Author: Even though I try to write what happens to Angela. There's no point: Angela is only a meaning. A stray meaning? She is the words I forgot.

Angela: I'm impersonal even in friendship, even in love.
    I'm an Anonymous Society. An open parenthesis. Please close me.
    Every being is some other being, undoubtedly one but brittle, unique fingerprints ad saecula saeculorum.

Author: She's always in a situation of at least semi-crisis. She applies intensity to things that don't deserve it. To everything she lends a passion that exceeds the reason for the passion. And the frivolity is in giving such importance to the foam of life. Once she's got something, she no longer desires it. Grabbing the moment is a synchrony between her and time: without hurry but without delay. An infinite present that neither leans toward the past nor projects itself toward the future. That is why she lives so much. Her life "doesn't change the subject," it's not interrupted by imaginary life. Imaginary life is living off the past or for the future. The present brings her pain. But this highly inexorable present casts a shadow where she can regain her strength, the warrior's repose. Emotional crisis.

She can't adapt to human beings. As though other beings existed, besides animals.

ANGELA: Oh sweet animal mystery. Oh gentle joy. So fascinating. So tremendously fascinating is this challenge of the beast! Oh sweet martyrdom of not knowing how to speak and only bark. You're the one who asks me if dying is sweet. I don't know either if dying is sweet. Until now I've only known the death of sleep. I kill myself every night.

Contact with animal life is indispensable to my psychic health. My dog reinvigorates me completely. Not to mention that he sometimes sleeps at my feet filling my bedroom with hot humid life. My dog teaches me to live. All he does is "be.""Being" is his activity. And being is my most profound intimacy. When he falls asleep in my lap I watch over him and his very rhythmical breathing. And—he motionless in my lap—we form a single organic being, a living mute statue. That is when I am moon and I am winds of the night. Sometimes, from so much mutual life, we trouble one another. My dog is as dog as a human is human. I love the doggishness and the hot humanity of both.

The dog is a mysterious animal because he almost thinks, not to mention that he feels everything except the notion of the future. The horse, unless he is winged, has his mystery resolved by nobility and a tiger is slightly more mysterious than the dog because its manner is even more primitive.

The dog—that misunderstood being who does whatever he can to share with men what he is …

AUTHOR: Angela's dog seems to have a person inside him. He is a person trapped by a cruel condition. The dog hungers so much for people and to be a man. A dog's inability to speak is excruciating.

If I could describe the inner life of a dog I would have reached a summit. Angela too wants to enter the being-alive of her Ulysses. I was the one who transmitted to her this love of animals.

ANGELA: Oh God, and here I am competing with myself. I detest myself. Fortunately others like me, it's a tranquility. My dog Ulysses and I are mutts. Ah what a good rain is falling. It's manna from heaven and only Ulysses and I know it. Ulysses drinks ice-cold beer so adorably. One of these days it's going to happen: my dog is going to open his mouth and speak. It'll be glory. Ulysses is Malta, he's Amapá—he's at the end of the world. How do you get there? He barks square—I'm not sure you're getting what I mean. During the world cup he went mad during the fireworks. And my head got all square. I try to understand my dog. He's the only innocent.

I can speak a language that only my dog, the esteemed Ulysses, my dear sir, understands. Like this: dacoleba, tutiban, ziticoba, letuban. Joju leba, leba jan? Tutiban leba, lebajan.

Atotoquina, zefiram. Jetobabe? Jetoban. That means something that not even the emperor of China would understand.

Once he did something unexpected. And I deserved it. I went to pet him, he growled. And I made the mistake of doing it again. He gave a sudden leap that rose up from his wild depths of the wolf and bit my mouth. I was terrified, I had to go to the emergency room where they gave me sixteen stitches. They told me to give Ulysses away because he was a danger. But it so happened that, after the accident, I felt even closer to him. Perhaps because he made me suffer. Suffering for a being deepens the heart within the heart.

AUTHOR: Angela and I are my inner dialogue—I talk to myself. I'm tired of thinking the same thoughts.

ANGELA: It's so wonderful and comforting to meet someone at four. Four p.m. is the best time of day. Four p.m. gives you balance and a calm stability, a serene taste for living. At times almost a bit whizzing and "in tremolo." So I become fluttering, iridescent and slightly excited.

AUTHOR: I must forgive Angela, once again, for this business about "the best time of the day." I must excuse her foolishness because she humbly knows her place: she knows she's not one of the elect and she's certainly not among the chosen. She knows that she will only be called and chosen once. When Death decides. Angela would rather it not be so. But, as for me, I'm already prepared and almost ready to be called. I realize it because of the disregard I feel for things and even for the act of writing. I find very little worthwhile now.

ANGELA: I bought a dress of black gauze with scattered flowers of a dead tone as though there were a veil over them putting them out. The whole dress seems to be played on a harp. I can feel myself flying in it, freed from the law of gravity. I'm ragged and weightless as though from black Africa I were resurging and arising white and pallid.

Black isn't a color, it's the absence of color.

AUTHOR: Angela is losing it. What do I care about the clothes she bought? She is sometimes an Austrian waltz. And when she speaks of God she becomes Bach. Moreover, she's hooked on possessing. She confuses possessing for living. That's why a dress can enrich her soul. Poor soul. She's vulgar. But she has one charming quality: she's a jug from which fresh water bubbles.

ANGELA: I'm suffering from happy love. That only seems like a contradiction. When you feel love, you have a deep anxiety. It's like I'm laughing and crying at the same time. Not to mention my fear that this happiness won't last. I have to be free — I can't stand the slavery of great love, love doesn't have such a hold on me. I can't submit to the pressure of the stronger force.

Where's my current of energy? my sense of discovery, though it takes an obscure form? I always expect something new from me, I am a shiver of expectation — something is always coming from me or from outside toward me.

AUTHOR: When Angela has a crisis of "womanishness" she spies on the world through the keyhole of the kitchen door. Her ambition is to live in a whirlpool of happiness. Stubborn without believing in life. I wonder if someone could simply decide: today is going to be an important day in my life. And then concentrate so much that the sun rises from within one's soul and the galaxies swirl slow and mute.

The drama of Angela is the drama of us all: balancing upon something unstable. For anything can happen and damage the most intimate life of a person. What will have been done to my soul next year? Will that soul have grown? and grown peacefully or through the pain of doubt?

ANGELA: A shot in the middle of the night.

All of a sudden I hear a shot. Or was it a tire that blew out? Did someone die? What a mystery, dear God. It's as if they were shooting me right into my poor heart.

Anyway, what poor thing! My heart is rich and strikes well the hours of my life.

The patience of the spider spinning the web. Moreover I'm bothered by badly making things out in the chiaroscuro of creation. I get skittish with the flash of inspiration. I am pure fear.

AUTHOR: I'd like to expose Angela to some terrifying music.

The music would have intervals of terrible silence with drops of flute-song here and there. Then a contralto voice suddenly and with extreme softness would hum with a closed mouth excessively calm and sure of itself: as in the threat that is made when one is sure of possessing deadly weapons. Angela would run and hide beneath the covers, holding on tightly to her dog Ulysses. I'm a little jealous of Ulysses. He's so important to Angela. And she doesn't seem grateful to me for having invented her. So I'll avenge myself with that terrifying music: a single note but repeated, repeated, repeated until near-madness. Angela fears madness and already thinks she's strange. I too find myself a bit strange but I don't fear madness:

I venture an icy lucidity. I see everything, I hear everything, I feel everything. And I stay far away from the intellectualized environments that would confound me. I am alone in the world. Angela is my only companion. You must understand me: I had to invent a being that was entirely mine. But it so happens that she's becoming too powerful.

ANGELA: I rarely scream. When I do scream it is a red and emerald scream. But in general I whisper. I speak quietly to tell timidly. Telling is very important. Telling the truth that covers itself in lies. How often I lie, my God. But it's to save myself. A lie is also a truth, it's just cunning and a little nervous. Lie if you can, and may you lie with a peaceful spirit. Because the truth demands a long staircase to climb as if I were condemned never to stop. I'm tired: that's also why I speak softly—it's so I don't offend myself.

AUTHOR: I'm an entangled and lost writer. Writing is difficult because it touches the boundaries of the impossible.

My head is full of characters but only Angela occupies my mental space.

ANGELA: It was intensely cold without any possible shelter. And the driver of the yellow cab had a bad cold. I forgot to say that, when I jumped out of the first taxi, in the middle of Avenida Rio Branco, people were crying out to me: I looked and saw everything that belonged to me exposed without blood on the asphalt of the street. And people were helping me in the middle of the traffic to gather my secrets. Because my purse had opened and been disemboweled: its entrails and my trampled prayers scattered across the ground. I gathered everything and stood humble and dignified waiting for who knows what. And while I was waiting a thin woman appeared and said, startling me: pardon me for asking, ma'am, but where did you buy that lovely green shawl? I was dismayed, and said to her defeated: I don't remember. Small unusual facts were happening to me, and I at their mercy.

AUTHOR: Angela is always becoming. Angela is my adventure. For that matter I am my own great adventure: I risk myself every instant. But there is a greater adventure: the God, I won't risk it.

ANGELA: I kept wandering aimlessly through the city. In the square the ones who give crumbs to the pigeons are the prostitutes and bums—more children of God than I. I give crumbs to you, my love. I, prostitute and bum. But with honor, folks, with my tribute to the pigeons. What a desire to do something wrong. The error is exciting. I'm going to sin. I'm going to confess something: sometimes, just for fun, I lie. I'm not at all what you think I am. But I respect the truth: I'm pure of sins.

Organ music is demonic. I want my life to be accompanied, as with twin sisters, by organ music. But it frightens me. Funeral music? I'm not sure, I'm a little out of it.

Today I killed a mosquito. With the most brutal sort of tact. Why? Why kill something that lives? I feel like a murderer and a guilty person. And I'll never forget that mosquito. Whose destiny I traced. The great killer. I, like an industrial crane, dealing with a delicate atom. Forgive me, little mosquito, forgive me, I'll never do it again. I think we have to do forbidden things—otherwise we suffocate. But without feeling guilty and instead as an announcement that we are free.

I'm my own mirror. And I live off the lost and found. That's what saves me. I'm caught in an invisible war between dangers. Who will win? I always lose.

AUTHOR: Angela is very provisional.

ANGELA: I can't manage to comprehend myself, no.
It's smoke in my eyes, it's the busy signal, it's the broken fingernail, scratch of chalk on the blackboard, it's the stuffy nose, it's suddenly rotten fruit, it's a speck in the eye, it's a kick in the butt, it's a stomp on the corn on my foot, it's a needle piercing my tender finger, it's a shot of Novocain, it's spit in my face.
I am a perfect actress.

AUTHOR: Crazy gazelle that she is.

ANGELA: My most intimate friend? A typewriter. There's a pleasant taste in my mouth when I think.

AUTHOR: She's a substantial beast.
I want your truth Angela! Just that: your truth that I can't quite grasp.

ANGELA: I love my feet: they obey me. And without doubting. The basic reason for my life is that there comes a time when I'm guided by a great hunger. That explains me. I'm indirect. I'm a person who is sudden and I get a little desperate when I think about the impossible. For example: I'll never manage to get a phone call from the emperor of Japan. I could be dying and he wouldn't call me. Or: how do you locate someone who isn't home? The impossible subdues me. I wither. Only last Sunday night—alone with my dog—my body joined my body. And then I was. I was I.

I'm hungry and sad. It's good to be a little sad. It's a sweet feeling. And it's good to be hungry and eat.

The most beautiful music in the world is the interstellar silence.

I'm sorry, but I can't be alone with you or else a star will be born in the air. Those who love solitude do not love freedom.

Flowers? flowers give such a fright. The perfect silence of a flower. Soft like turning off the light to go to sleep. And the light switch makes a little noise that seems to say: good night my love.

Ah, I'm filled with desire! I want to eat salmon and drink coffee. And cake. Everything's no more than a grand comedy that looks like a kermis. I want to be part of the festival of animals. In the shadows the rustling garden. The garden-abettor. Hiding-place of sparrows. Secrecy. The garden played on the harp ... Creative intumescence.

I was alone for a whole Sunday. I didn't call anyone and no one called me. I was completely alone. I sat on my sofa with my mind free. But as the day went on toward bedtime I experienced about three times a sudden recognition of myself and of the world that spooked me and made me plunge into obscure depths which I departed for golden light. It was the encounter of the I with the I. Solitude is a luxury.

AUTHOR: I looked for you in dictionaries and couldn't find your meaning. Where is your synonym in the world? where is my own synonym in life? I'm unequalled.

ANGELA: In some modern music a precise note of heroic classicism is missing.

AUTHOR: You're missing a certain extravagance, you don't have a way of treating others more generously. You are the literal meaning.

ANGELA: I thought of something so beautiful that I couldn't even understand it. And I ended up forgetting what it was.

AUTHOR: I love you geometrically and at a point on the horizon forming a triangle with you. The result is a perfume of macerated roses.

ANGELA: Pain? Happiness? It's simply a matter of opinion.
   I divine things that have no name and perhaps never shall. Yes. I sense things that will always be inaccessible to me. Yes. But I know everything. All that I know without exactly knowing it has no synonym in the world of speech but enriches me and justifies me. Although I lost the word because I tried to speak it. And knowing-everything-without-knowing is a perpetual forgetting that comes and goes like the waves of the sea that advance and recede on the sands of the beach. To civilize my life is to expel me from myself. To civilize my deepest existence would be to try to expel my nature and supernature. All of this meanwhile does not address my possible meaning.
   What kills me is the day-to-day. I only wanted exceptions. I'm lost: I have no habits.

AUTHOR: Angela has all this fairy-like illumination—and while she grows accustomed slow and mute and majestic and extremely delicate and fatal—to being a woman—she's too modest for it, too fleeting to be defined. She told me that once on the street she approached an officer—and explained that she did so because he should know about things and to top it off was armed, which filled her with respect. So she said to the officer: sir, could you tell me, if you please, when does spring-time begin?

Angela is mad. But she has a mathematical logic in her apparent madness. And she has a lot of fun, that scandalous creature. She gets too keen and then doesn't know what to do with herself. To hell with her. Between the "yes" and the "no" there is only one way: choosing. Angela chose "yes." She is so free that one day she'll end up in jail. "In jail for what?" "For excessive freedom." "But isn't that freedom innocent?" "Yes. Even naive." "So why prison?" "Because freedom offends."

I wanted to defend Angela with strong Swiss military guards, so sinful is she, so much does she squander her life. Yet she's happy as a military march.

ANGELA: I am an "actress," I appear, say what I know then exit the stage. What more could such a rich person want who has a highly intelligent mechanism like a supercomputer?

AUTHOR: I'm worrying too much about Angela's life and forgetting my own. I became am abstraction of myself: I'm a sign, I symbolize something that exists more than I do, I'm in the category of things that can't be categorized.

ANGELA: Presence of princes, Amazons, Vikings, Atlantises, sprites, fauns, gnomes, mothers, prostitutes, giants, all with lips painted black and green nails. Roots tangled and angled, exposed, immobilization by the pain of having grown.

AUTHOR: She sometimes sees reality, a reality more invented and that never comes close to the truth, as if that entirely naked truth would frighten her. She is a superlative. She pretends she's happy, but sometimes that happiness disturbs her.

ANGELA: I come from a long longing. I, who am praised and adored. But nobody wants anything to do with me. My irrepressible spirit frightens anyone who might come along. With a few exceptions, everyone's scared of me as though I might bite. Neither I nor Ulysses bites. We're gentle and happy, and sometimes we bark in anger or fear. I hide my failure from myself. I give up. And sadly I collect expressions of love. In Portuguese it's "eu te amo." In French — "je t'aime." In English — "I love you." In Italian — "io t'amo." In Spanish — "yo te quiero." In German — "Ich liebe disch," is that right? Me of all people, the unloved. The most disappointed one of all, she who every night tastes the sweetness of death.

I feel like a charlatan. Why? It's as if I weren't revealing my final truth. So I have to take off my clothes and be naked in the street. That's not so hard. But what's hard is to have a naked soul. So I give myself to God. And I pray a lot that protection might be granted me. Am I from another planet? what am I? the humblest of the humble who is prostrate on the ground and presses her half-open mouth to the earth in order to suck its blood. Oh earth, but what a scent of wet grass. How comforting it is. And I also undress in the sea. Could it be I'll have a tragic end? Oh please spare me. Please: because I am fragile. What awaits me when I die? I already know: when I die I'll go transparent as jade.

AUTHOR: Angela is afraid to travel for fear of losing her I during the trip. She needs for at least one minute in her life to catch herself in the act. To catch what's living and take her immobile picture and look at herself in the picture and think that the snapshot left a proof, that of the already-dead picture.

ANGELA: Suddenly an odd feeling. I find myself odd as though a movie camera were filming my steps and suddenly stopped, leaving me immobile in the middle of a gesture: caught in the act. Me? Am I the one who is I? But this is a mad senselessness! Part of me is mechanical and automatic—neurovegetative, the balance between not wanting and wanting, of not being able and being able, all of it sliding along in the routine of mechanism. The camera singled out the instant. And so it is that I automatically left myself in order to capture myself dazed by my own enigma, right there before me, which is unprecedented and terrifying because it's extremely true, profoundly naked life merged into my identity. And this encounter between life and my identity forms a miniscule unbreakable and radiant indivisible diamond, a single atom and all of me feels my body go numb as when you stay in the same position for a long time and your leg suddenly "falls asleep."

I am too nostalgic, I seem to have lost something who knows where or when.

AUTHOR: I shall write here toward the air and responding to nothing because I am free. I—I who exist. There's a voluptuousness in being someone. I am no longer silence. I feel so impotent while living—life that sums up all the disparate and dissonant opposites in a single and ferocious stance: rage.

I finally reached the nothing. And in my satisfaction at having reached in myself the minimum of existence, only the necessary breathing—I am therefore free. All that's left for me is to invent. But I immediately warn myself: I'm uncomfortable. Uncomfortable for myself. I feel ill at ease in this body that is my baggage. But that discomfort is the first step toward my— toward my what? truth? As if I had the truth?

I say nothing like real music does. It doesn't speak words. I feel no longing for myself—what I was no longer interests me! And if I should speak, may I allow myself to be discontinuous: I have no obligation to myself. I go on accumulating myself, accumulating myself, accumulating myself—until I no longer fit within me and burst into words.

When I write, I mix one color with another, and a new color is born.

I want to forget that I never forgot. I want to forget the praise and the jeers. I want to re-inaugurate myself. And for that I'll have to renounce my whole body of work and begin humbly, without deificaton, from a beginning in which there are no traces of any habit, foibles or abilities. I'll have to put aside my know-how. For that reason I expose myself to a new kind of fiction, which I still don't even know how to handle.

The main thing I want to reach is to surprise myself with what I write. To be assaulted: to tremble before what was never said by me. To fly low in order not to forget the ground. To fly high and wildly in order to let loose my great wings. Up until now I feel like I've never really taken flight. This book, I suspect, won't let me fly either despite my desire to. Because nothing will be decided in this matter, in this matter all that counts is what happens when it comes from the nothing. But the worst thing is that the thought in the word has already been spent. Each loose word is a thought stuck to it like flesh to a nail.

ANGELA: I am what's beyond thought. I write in the state of drowsiness, only a slight contact with what I'm living within myself and also an inter-relational life. I act like a sleepwalker. The next day I don't recognize what I wrote. I only recognize my own handwriting. And I find a certain charm in the freedom of phrases, not worrying much about an apparent disconnection. Phrases have no interference from time. They could happen in the next century just as they could have happened in the last, with small superficial variations.

Could my individuality be dead?

AUTHOR: Everything goes by in a daydream: real life is a dream. I don't need to "understand" myself. That I can vaguely feel, is enough for me. When I think without any thought — I call that meditation. And it's so profound that I can't quite reach and words disappear, manifestations. I meditate, and what emerges from that meditation has nothing to do with meditation: an idea comes that seems totally disconnected from the meditation. It seems it's only useful to live interrogatively since every interrogation tossed into the air has a corresponding reply formed in the darkness of my being, that part of me which is dark and vital, without it I'd be empty. Whenever I do something deliberately nothing comes out, therefore I get distracted almost deliberately. I pretend I don't want something, I end up believing I don't want it and only then does the thing come.

Things happen indirectly. They come sideways. I'd swear it's from the left side. (I get on better with my left side.) Which is battered like a look of sensitive melancholic tenderness. It's the encounter between purity and purity and so we feel we're allowed it, I don't know what else to say. So — I don't say it or maybe it would be better for me to say it. To be a being allowed to yourself is the glory of existing. To be able to say to yourself with shame and awkwardly: it's you, too, you I love, a bit. I allow myself. Then I reach the ultra-sonorous. The one speaking, it seems to be me, but I'm not. It's a "she" that speaks in me.

Sometimes I'm dense like Beethoven, other times I'm Debussy, strange and light melody. All accompanied by a breathing, three movements and pouring out from four wonders. My dream is accompanied by a breathing and by three instants from which seven wonders pour. I walk atop and along the sound of a single prolonged note. The translucent green morning with the chirping of hundreds of little birds still has something of the dark night's nightmare: a dog barks in the harsh morning off in the distance.

As I was saying: it was God who invented me. And so too do I—as in the Greek Olympiads the athletes who ran passed forward the burning torch—so too do I use my breath and invent Angela Pralini and make her a woman. A beautiful woman.

Angela and I are my interior dialogue: I talk to myself. Angela is from my dark interior: she however comes to light. The tenebrous darkness from which I emerge. Pullulating darkness, lava of a humid volcano burning intensely. Darkness full of worms and butterflies, rats and stars.

I think in hieroglyphs (mine). And in order to live I must constantly interpret myself and each time the key to the hieroglyph, I'm sure that the dream—thing (mine) (worthless), not carried through—is the key to the same.

I write in words that hide others—the true ones. Because the true words cannot be named. Even if I don't know which are the "true words," I am always alluding to them. My spectacular and ongoing failure proves that the opposite exists: success. Even if success is not granted me, I'm satisfied to know it exists.

Occasionally I myself am writing this book.

So I'll talk about the problems of writing. About the vortex which is placing oneself in a creative state. I feel that I have a triple star.

I, the author of this book, am being possessed by a thousand demons writing inside me. This need to flow, ah, never, never to stop flowing. If that source that exists within each of us stops it's horrible. The source is of mysteries, hidden mysteries and if it stops that is because death is coming. I'm trying in this book a bit crazy, a bit ostentatious, a bit dancing naked in the streets, a bit the clown, a bit the fool at the court of the king. I, the king of sleep, I only know how to sleep and eat, I learned nothing else. As for the rest, ladies and gentlemen, I hold my tongue. I just won't tell you the secret of life because I still haven't learned it. But one day I shall be the secret of life. Each of us is the secret of life and the one is the other and the other is the one.

I must not forget the Franciscan modesty of the sweetness of a little bird. Speak marvelous things ah ye who wish to write life long or short as it may be. It is a cursed profession that gives no rest. I don't know if it's the dream that makes me write or if the dream is the result of a dream that comes from writing. Are we full or hollow? Who art thou who readest me? Art thou my secret or am I thy secret?

With a poor life (and what is a rich life?), with life poor I escape from it through the imaginary. But my imaginary doesn't happen through actions but through the feeling-thinking that is actually a dream. I imagine marvelous words and I receive from them their dazzle. The word "topaz" transports me to the deepest part of my dream: topaz fascinates me in its luminous abyss of real stone. Once I dreamed there was a reality: it happened when I pondered the mute enigma of the dreamt reality that exists in topaz.

In the act of writing I attain here and now the most secret dream, the one I can't remember when I wake up. In what I write the only thing that interests me is finding my timbre. My timbre of life.

I love Angela Pralini because she allows me to sleep while she speaks. I who sleep for a certain preparative experience of death. A beginner's course because death is so incommensurable that I shall be lost within it. No—to speak sincerely—I can't allow the world to exist after my death. My regrets to those I leave behind alive and watching television, regrets because humanity and the human condition are guilty without absolution for my death.

ANGELA: At night the dead walk the paths of the old cemetery and no one hears their cymbals. A clarinet goes out of tune sharp and mute. I tremble in my bed with a chill that shakes me and doesn't. I don't scream. No. But I am barely alive. I'm nothing but a stifled breath. I think low and slow-moving: if I am alive it's because I shall die. The clarinet plays again. And now I'm going to turn out the light and sleep.

AUTHOR: (While Angela sleeps.) All the words written here can be summed up by an ever-present state I call "I am being."

ANGELA: Not long ago I saw a slice of watermelon on the table. And, there on the naked table, it looked like a madman's laugh (I don't know how else to put it). If I weren't resigned to living in a world that forces me to be sensible, how I would scream in fright at the happy prehistoric monstrosities of the earth. Only an infant isn't shocked: he too is a happy monstrosity repeated since the beginning of the history of man. Only afterwards does fear come, the pacification of fear, the denial of fear—in a word, civilization. Meanwhile, atop the naked table, the screaming slice of red watermelon. I am grateful to my eyes that are still so frightened. I shall yet see many things. To be honest, even without watermelon, a naked table is also a sight to see.

AUTHOR: I write as if I were sleeping and dreaming: phrases disconnected as in a dream. It's difficult, being awake, to dream freely about my remote mysteries. There is a coherence—but only in the depths. For someone on the surface and not dreaming the phrases mean nothing. Although even awake some know they are living in a dream within real life. What is real life? the facts? no, real life is only reached through that part of real life that's dreamt.

Dreaming is not an illusion. But it is the act that a person does alone.

I—I want to break the limits of the human race and become free to the point of the wild or "divine" cry.

But I feel defenseless before the world that is then open to me. Who? who will accompany me in this solitude whose summit I, if it weren't for you, Angela, would never reach? Or perhaps I'm wanting to enter the most remote mysteries that while I'm asleep only emerge in dreams.

Imagination precedes reality! Except I only know how to imagine words. I only know one thing: I am pungently real. And that I am alive photographing the dream. Anyone can daydream as long you don't keep your consciousness too brightly lit.

My life is attempting to conquer that Unknown. Because God is from another world—the great ghost.

Real life is a dream, but with open eyes (that see everything distorted). Real life enters us in slow motion, including the most rigorous rationality—it's a dream. Consciousness is only useful to me for knowing that I live fumbling around and in the (only apparent) illogic of the dream. The dream of the wakeful is real matter. We are such illogical dreamers that we count on the future. I base my life upon the waking dream. What guides me is the project by which tomorrow comes to be tomorrow. My freedom? my own freedom is not free: it runs on invisible rails. Not even madness is free. But it's also true that freedom without a directive would be a butterfly flying in the air. But in the dreams of the wakeful there's an inconsequential lightness of a brook, bubbling and coherent. The state of being.

What I dream at night and forget the next morning—that intimate discomfort of someone who ignores part of his life: death escapes me. Sometimes I don't sleep all night hoping to dream while I'm awake and to be conscious of the mystery and depths of the dream. And actually, even without sleeping, out of fatigue, I start to daydream.

I am an abyss of myself. But I shall always be aslant. And the white horses fill my pupils with burning love. I own seven purebred horses. Six white and one black.

Daily life contains within itself the abuse of daily life: daily life has the tragedy of the tedium of repetition. But there's a loophole: that the great reality is exceptional, like a dream in the entrails of the day.

I've never had a vocation for writing: the number is what fascinated me since I was a boy. If now I daily and clumsily make notes, it's because my wife's no good at conversation.

I used to try to write and thought it was fun, it's an adventure, I never know what will happen to me in the form of words and what I'll discover from day to day for my own good, I'll do everything possible not to use the technical vocabulary that comes to me naturally because I studied physics.

ANGELA (*Depth: somnambulism*): Good morning and good afternoon and good night for whenever you like, oh charging rhinoceros and I must be careful with you. I'll say it like this: careful-careful-careful. Careful with the high sky, it can come down and entangle me in mists and blue and my wings will fly in blind flight up into those dense mists of the blue that is not transparent because the blue of the sky is not transparent and in it are encrusted the stars, but the sun and the moon are in front of the blue, the blue is behind the sun and the moon, and the sun and the moon swim above in the air without color. What separates me from the blue of the high sky are the absolute kilometers of air without color and the air without color is round and is what I breathe, I don't breathe the blue sky. And when you put your cold hand in mine, I, the warm one, feel a shiver down my spine and I kill, kill, kill you until you are completely dead and of no use to any other woman, again I kill, kill and kill you. I don't want you at all, "mister" cold-hand. I'll go off in search of a warm hand, and send you my true love back to the bitch that bore you, there's a disturbing gap between us—that's why I'm thinking of filling this gap and I have a lover to favor you and save you from the empty and hollow bottomless gap that is the void. What I'm writing now is meant for no one: it's directly meant for writing itself, this writing consumes writing. This, my book of the night, nourishes me with a cantabile melody. What I write is autonomously real.

I want the thinking-feeling now and, no, to have it only had yesterday or going to have it tomorrow. I'm in a certain hurry to feel everything. I don't want anything to get lost in the passage from the I-mine to the I-global. I want to reach within myself a landscape deep beneath the earth a spring of placid waters running—and my ecstatic soul that can't be restrained and trembles in the lightest orgasm. Pure contemplation.

I never saw anything more solitary than having a new and original idea. Not if you're supported by no one and barely believe in yourself. The newer the sensation-idea, the closer you seem to the solitude of madness. When I have a new sensation it thinks I'm strange and I think it's strange. I also can't stand the piercing and lonely happiness of feeling happy. I lack the serenity to accept good news. When I get happy, I become nervous and agitated. The light shimmers too brightly for my poor eyes.

AUTHOR: As a profession I wanted to be the one who rings the bells (but not to call the faithful). With what joy I myself would tremble at the translucent, potent and echoing vibrations in the air of life: vigorous ecstatic tolling. It is a sound even more splendid than Bach.

But my kingdom is not the clamorous transparency of the soul of the bells. To the contrary: tenebrous I feed off the black bitter roots of the trees, reaching them by digging into the earth with knotty hard fingers and dirty nails: I eat and chew and swallow the earth.

What am I saying! It is or isn't the truth. I lie so much that I write. I lie so much that I live. I lie so much that I seek the truth of me. You will be my truth. I want the truthful seed of you. If I manage to cross the dense forest of deceptions. I'm a blunder in a labyrinth made of the bloody threads of nerves. And I don't understand what you're saying, Angela, I only understand what you're thinking. Wanting to understand is one of the worst things that could happen to me. But through your innocence I am learning not to know. But I live in danger. Not the danger of facts but something more urgent ...

ANGELA (*Somnambulism*): Dark gray your eyes of steel that fascinate me your mouth of edges lighter than your lips. You only embrace me too strongly when you want to but never guess when I want to.

Grapes, a bunch of grapes round and fleshy and liquid and

falsely transparent because they give the impression of being transparent, but you can't see the other side you are entirely opaque though you give the impression of transparency what the hell do I have to do with the opacity of things and yours the bull on the ranch is stocky the cows smelling of pastures and unheard-of pastures the pasture lies in the open air between pasture and sky I breathe the air that flies flies lightly when it starts to blow gently against my naked and uncontrolled crazy face when the windows bang and bang the gusts of winds I really like being touched by the wind as I like to expose myself to the gusts that bang against the doors and windows of the entire house. They bang and bang fast crazy we and the servants run to shut them and inside the shut mansion we suffocate in dying electric light listening to the whine of the violent and quick wind the shut doors and windows shake.

It's said like this kissed by the cliché breeze I prefer to say that the breeze blesses me between slightly ochre and at the same time lightly astringent it's also lightly sweet on lips that are polluted by the pollen brought by the veil of perfume that is the breeze.

AUTHOR: Angela, who knows why she had this idea: to count numbers from one to a thousand. And something in fact happens: as the numbers go higher, she herself reaches a state of extreme grace, so rarefied it's almost unbreathable. It happens like a somnambulist hypnosis but with a slight touch of consciousness: just enough for her to be aware of herself. And to know she's being carried off by her own self—all of a sudden, a stranger—to a realm full of fables.

Angela is a dream of mine.

I'm sleepy-headed and the words flow out of me coming

from a flux that is not mental. Empty the way you get when you reach the purest state of thinking. To sprout into thought is very exciting, sensual. Though sometimes sultry weather, sun behind the clouds. As for me, I keep my strange power a secret. I'm not sure what kind of power—part darkness and perhaps of some strength. Who knows if that power is summed up in breathing? in thinking? in almost foreseeing? in being able to kill and not killing? It's a contained power. Sometimes the thought that springs up tickles me because it's so light and inexpressible. I have thoughts I cannot translate into words—sometimes I think a triangle. But when I try to think I get worried about trying to think and nothing comes up. Sometimes my thought is only the whispering of my leaves and branches. But for my best thought words are not found.

I discovered that I need to not know what I'm thinking—if I become conscious of what I'm thinking, I can no longer think, I can only see myself think. When I say "think" I'm referring to the way I dream words. But thought needs to be a feeling.

I now know how to think of nothing. It was a conquest. Not thinking means the inexpressible contact with the Nothing. The "Nothing" is the beginning of a free availability that Angela would call Grace.

ANGELA: I had insomnia last night.

I closed my eyes relaxed my body and tried not to think so I could fall asleep. Little by little I started having a strange awareness of abandonment. My (thought?) my essence was … My body was beside me and I saw it transparent and through the transparency pulsing arteries, living, full of blood that circulated as quickly as possible through all of my limbs: they looked like irrigation channels. I also saw air, water and a yellow liquid.

I could see everything in full color. Everything in absolute silence. Not everyone is given the fleeting plunge into one's own mysterious flesh. This body of mine that is autonomous and surely electronic. No machine makes me live. My body is alive and works like a factory working in absolute silence. My interior is one of the strangest and most beautiful things in the world. I am brilliant Nature. Only God, who is creative energy, could have made me with the perfection of the treasure that I have inside me. Afterwards my thought or visionary essence returned to me and that return was very comfortable and I felt fully satisfied. And with a delicate tenderness for possessing that inexplicable thing that worked for me. I don't remember anything else. Right afterwards I felt a drowsiness slowly taking me over and I fell asleep beneath the blessing of the body of God.

AUTHOR: Angela thinks that the state of grace or of life lies in making the most of oneself in the external world. She even strives to conquer God, making Him the external world. But the one who lives in a state of grace, not permanently but with great frequency, is me. I managed this through a disinterest in the world. I live an emptiness that is also called fullness. Not having heaps blessings upon me. As for my practical life I managed to live in a big and turbulent city as if it were provincial and easy.

Angela writes the way she lives: projecting herself. But I am already free: I write for nothing. I clear a path for myself. I live without models. I write without models. Being free is what gives me that great responsibility.

I … I … I?

Angela: As for me, I'm cautious but I'm not stupid. To-night—blustery—I dreamt such a gratifying dream. There was a boy of 14 and a girl of 13 who were running after one another, hiding behind trees, and bursting out laughing, play-ing. And suddenly they stopped and mute, serious, frightened looked into one another's eyes: because they knew one day they would love.

Author: Angela is urgent and emergent. As a judge I am unfortunately more tied to the slow than I'd wish.

Here I am. I was enlisted and I introduce myself to myself. And a drop of gold falls. Reality is more unattainable than God—because you cannot pray to reality.

In the dream of the real it seems it's not me I'm living but somebody else. That other person is Angela who is my day-dream.

Am I speaking or is Angela speaking?

Reality does not exist in itself. What there is is seeing the truth through the dream. Real life is merely symbolic: it refers to something else.

Action—that is the aim of the sorcerer! The sorcerer tries to substitute himself for the Law, either for his own benefit, or for the benefit of the person who employs and pays him.

I wouldn't exist if there were no words.

Angela goes from language to existence. She wouldn't exist if there were no words.

I've been a writer a long time, and I can only say that the more you write the harder it gets. Am I competing against my-self? For example, I've been wanting to write about a person I invented: a woman named Angela Pralini. And it's difficult. How to separate her from me? How do I make her different from what I am? One thing's for sure and it's no use trying to change it: Angela inherited from me the desire to write and to paint. And if she inherited that part of me, it's because I can't imagine a life without the art of writing or painting or making music. What does Angela want from life? Little by little I'll find out. At the same time I'll find out what I want from life. It's just that Angela is propelled by ambition and I by a chaste humility. To write I can't lose sight of my paltry ability. I am a low musical note. Angela is a high note, she's a cry in the air. I whisper, Angela, with a clear, high and limpid voice, sings her futilities that have the gift of looking like profound and fantastic realities. I lost my style: which I consider a gain: the less style I have, the purer the naked word that emerges. I must, in my solitude, confide in someone and that's why I made Angela be born: I want to maintain a dialogue with her. But it so happens that, in pages predating these, in written pages I already tore up, I stated that my dialogue with Angela is a dialogue of the deaf: one of us says something and the other says yes but in response to something else, and then I come along saying no, and I see Angela's not even contradicting me. Each of us follows a different thread in the plot, without really hearing the other very much. That is freedom. And I can't complain: I myself gave Angela this freedom and independence. She almost always ignores me. I fight to maintain my style whatever that is and of which the critics have not yet purified me. — Angela fights to create her own way of expressing herself. So, because in a certain sense I am her owner—I force her to write simply. Angela—how can I explain—has a golden anxiety. I have the weight of an anguish in my chest, anguish without gold or crystal or silver. Angela is sun-gold, she's glittering-diamond, she's reflecting crystal. I also imagine her like an enormous emerald sparkling in the void of the air and her deep transparent green is magical. She is a waterfall of precious stones. I envy her, I who variably lose my opacity.

ANGELA: I came up against the impossible of myself.

At that point, I went off key without meaning to. Unreal like music. I, sleepy and phantasmagoric in deepest night filled with smoke and we surrounding the bright yellowish lamp, light that will not let me sleep, like the intense spotlights that torturers shine on their victims to not let them rest.

I used to be a woman who knew how to make things out when I saw them. But now I committed the grave error of thinking.

AUTHOR: Angela lives stunned in great disorder. If not for me, Angela wouldn't be conscious. If not for me, she'd be diaphanous like the perfume of a dream. For her to be more than the perfume of a dream I scatter across her vastness a hard cactus here, some more over there. Like milestones. Perfume of a dream? but she's the immaterial substratum of me.

ANGELA: I'm like a sleepwalker. I want to compose a symphony whose scenario includes silence—and the audience wouldn't clap because they would sense that the motionless musicians—as in a photograph—didn't mean to say "the end." The music is at its peak—then there's a minute of silence—and the sounds start again.

AUTHOR: Besides my involuntary but incisive role of poor scribbler—besides that is the silence that invades all the interstices of my total darkness.

Music deeply teaches me a boldness in the world to feel itself. I seek disorder, I seek the primitive state of chaos. That is where I feel myself living. I need the darkness that implores, the receptivity of the most primary forms of wanting.

The small success of my books made it hard for me to write. I was invaded by the words of others. I must reencounter my difficulty. It comes from what is true in me. I must free myself of skills. These skills allow me to write even for the semi-literate. For I don't even need myself. I'm free of myself. Terribly idle because I need nothing else. Not even the next day.

What sustains and balances a man are his little hang-ups and habits. And they enhance his development because whatever is repeated often enough ends up deepening a demeanor and allowing it space. But in order to experience any sort of surprise the routine of habits and hang-ups must be for whatever reason suspended. What am I left with? With critical depth or a stimulating surprise? I believe I'm left with both, anarchically intermingled or simultaneous. Simultaneity in creative work comes from deepening: sometimes, digging deep into the earth you suddenly see a sparkle—an unexpected gem.

I use the banking system and do not understand it. I use the telephone and do not comprehend its mechanism. I turn on the television and all I know about television is how to turn it on. I use man and do not know him. I use myself and …

ANGELA: … and I see everything with new perspectives: the table where I write stretches beyond the length of a table, my pen is enormously long and I must in order to write keep myself far from the table so that the tip of the pen can reach the paper that is whiter than paper. From the lampshade gushes a great triangle of light upon the paper and my hand and I make a huge shadow on the wall. Everything got larger. I, the paper, the light and the pen are free in the boundless field where golden wheat grows.

AUTHOR: I, alchemist of myself. Am I a man who devours himself? No, it's that I live in eternal mutation, with new adaptations to my renewed living and I never reach the end of any of the ways of existing. I live from unfinished and vacillating sketches. But I try my best to balance between me and I, between me and others, between me and the God.

I live in darkness of the soul, and my heart beating, eager for future pulsations that cannot stop. But the occasional phrase escapes the shadows and rises light and volatile to my surface: then I note it here.

But what I wanted was to bring to my surface the rich darkness itself that would be like petroleum gushing dark and thick and rich.

I am not an informer but sometimes I happen to give news that surprises even me.

When I concentrate I concentrate without meaning to and without knowing how I manage to but I manage independent of myself. Or better yet: it happens. But when I myself want to concentrate then I distract myself and lose myself in the "wanting" and end up only feeling the wanting that comes to be the goal. And the concentration doesn't happen. The desire must be hidden to not kill the vital nerve of what you wanted.

Who orders me around, if not me? For I can't manage to reach myself.

What is the word that represents the "unknown" that we feel within ourselves? I've adhered to the unknown for a long time now. What is the reality of the world? because I don't know. Nature is not casual. For it repeats itself, and repeated accidents become a law, those accidents that are not accidents.

I'm horrified and my brow is covered with cold sweat. Because if what I can barely sense really is true—then I must radically change my life.

What am I thinking? okay, I'll try to explain with humid brow and slightly shaking hand: here goes:

Perhaps—perhaps whatever is correct lies precisely in error? If that's true, how many fruitful "errors" I have lost. That would contradict everything I learned and everything human society taught me. Fearing the error, I degraded myself. To avoid the error, I ventured nothing great. I, standing in the street, cast a shadow on the ground. My shadow is my opposite of the "correct," my shadow is my error—and that shadow-error belongs to me, only I possess it inside me, I am the only person in the world whose lot it was to be me. So is there an acquired right to be me? And now I want my errors back. I reclaim them.

I want to forget that readers exist—and demanding readers too who hope for I don't know what from me. So I'll take my freedom into my hands and write I-don't-care-what?, truly awful, but me.

I am only sporadically. The rest is empty words, they too sporadic.

An attempt to sensitize the language so that it shivers and shakes and my earthquake opens frightening fissures in this free language—but I captive and in the process of not being I become aware and it goes on without me.

To get things started, let me assure you that you only live, real life, when you learn that even the lie is true. I decline to offer proof. But if someone insists on the "whys," I'll answer:

the lie is born in the person who creates it and it brings into existence new lies from new truths.

One word is the lie of another.

I demandingly want you to believe me. I want you to believe me even when I lie.

ANGELA: I'm not—I hope—judging myself with excessive impartiality. But I need to be a bit impartial or else I succumb and get tangled in my pathetic form of living. Besides physically there's something rather pathetic about me: my big eyes are childishly interrogative at the same that they seem to ask for something and my lips are always half-open like when you're surprised or when the air you breathe through your nose is insufficient and so you breathe through your mouth: or the way lips look when they are about to be kissed. I am, without being aware of it, a trap.

Though I am wise, I don't really understand what's happening to me. And the world demanding decisions from me for which I am not prepared. Decisions not only about provoking the birth of facts but also decisions about the best way to be.

A tension of the string of a violin.

I don't understand my remotest past, childhood and adolescence which lives without understanding and without paying attention. I was giddy. Now without the slightest support at the foundation of my life I am loose and perilous and events come at me like something always discontinuous, not connected to a previous understanding to which these events would be an intelligible succession. But no: events don't seem to have their cause in me. I don't properly understand what's happening to me. And my point of view regarding honors is primary.

Why do I want to make a hero of myself? I in fact am anti-heroic. What torments me is that everything is "for the time being," nothing is "always." Life—from the moment you're born—is guided, idealized by dreams. I plan nothing, I leap into the darkness and chew upon shadows, and in these shadows I sometimes see the luminous and pure sparkling of three inedible diamonds. So I rise to the surface with a diamond in each pupil of my eyes in order to pass through the opacity of the world and another between my half-closed lips so that when I speak my words will be crystalline, hard and dazzling.

AUTHOR: I wanted a very delicate, schizoid, elusive true kind of writing that would reveal to me the unwrinkled face of eternity. Obsessed with the desire to be happy I lost my life. I moved with the tension of a bow and arrow in an unreality of desires.

ANGELA: What's missing in my writing is the dream. How secret living is! My secret is life. I tell no one I'm alive.

AUTHOR: We're living at the fin de siècle, wasting away in decadence—or are we in the Golden Age? we're on the verge of an unfolding. On the verge of knowing ourselves. On the verge of the year 2000.

The world? Its merciless and tragic history is my past. Could it be that the word topaz has already been drained of its thought? No, I still feel the shining of an energy in the translucent golden word called topaz.

I'm a beggar with a beard full of lice seated on the sidewalk crying. I'm no more than that. I'm neither happy nor sad. I'm exempt and unscathed and gratuitous.

ANGELA: To sleep … With my heart all shut and unsteady, my hand shaking, the intimate warmth of a sip of red wine. And getting into a bed full of pillows and choosing the best position. Then a murmur of prayer comes from my warm blood. But I never can capture the zero-instant when I fall asleep and sleeping I die.

It's night and I went barefoot through the shadowy sands but the sea was a thick outpouring of the dark night—and I was scared like a little swallow. The black sea was calling me in the undertow of the low tide, black surf.

After hardly sleeping all night I'm in a state of rustic vigilance. And what my dreams should have been if I had slept at night started happening by day: in any case these dreams turned up and had to simply had to pass even through narrow gaps that the day opens within me. So it's impossible for me to stop dreaming and letting my mind wander. I'm a skull that's hollow and with vibrating walls and full of bluish clouds: they are the matter of sleeping and dreaming and not of being. I must simply must invent my future and invent my path.

I want the shining gravel in the dark brook. I want the sparkle of the stone beneath the rays of sun, I want death that frees me. I could manage to have pleasure if I abstained from thinking. Then I'd feel the ebb and flow of air in my lungs. I try to live without past without present and without future and here I am free.

It is morning. The world is as happy as an abandoned circus.

AUTHOR: It's a very pretty day. There's a misty rain, the sky is dark and the sea turbulent. Souls flutter about the cemetery, vampires are on the loose, bats huddle in their caves. Refuge for mystery and terror. If suddenly the sun appeared I would give a cry of astonishment and a world would crumble and there wouldn't even be time for everyone to flee the brightness. The beings who feed on shadows.

I'm only interested in writing when I surprise myself with what I write. I can do without reality because I can have everything through thought.

Reality doesn't surprise me. But that's not true: I suddenly feel such a hunger for the "thing to really happen" that I cry out and bite into reality with my lacerating teeth. And afterwards give a sigh over the captive whose flesh I ate. And again, for a long while, I do without real reality and find comfort in living from my imagination.

*How Can You Transform
Everything into a Daydream?*

AUTHOR: The fact is more important than the text.

Facts trip me up. That is why I am now going to write about not-facts, that is, about things and their gaudy mystery.

The sensation of writing is curious. When I write I'm not thinking about the reader or myself: then I am—but only from me—I am the words strictly speaking.

ANGELA: I like words. Sometimes a random and scentillating phrase occurs to me, without having anything to do with the rest of me. From now on I'm going to write in this diary, on days when there's nothing else to do, phrases almost on the edge of meaninglessness but that sound like words of love. Saying meaningless words is my great freedom. It matters little to me to be understood, I want the impact of dazzling syllables, I want the noxiousness of a bad word. Everything is in the word. What I'd give, however, not to have this mistaken desire to write. I feel like I'm being pushed. By whom?

I want to write with words so completely stuck together that there are no gaps between them and me.

I want to write really angry. As for me, I'm from far away. Very far. And from me comes the pure smell of kerosene.

AUTHOR: The word is the defecation of the thought. It glistens.

Every book is blood, it's pus, it's excrement, it's heart torn to shreds, it's nerves cut to pieces, it's electric shock, it's coagulated blood running like boiling lava down the mountain.

ANGELA: Oh I no longer want to express myself with words: I want to do so with "I-kiss-you."

AUTHOR: I occasionally, I who am writing, seek for every word the unconscious pop of a mortifying feeling.

ANGELA: I want to write and can't do it. I want to write a story called: "A Foot." And another called: "You're So Severe." In what I write is there nothing between the lines? If that's the case, I'm lost.

The novel I want to write would be "It's Like Trying to Remember. And Not Being Able."

"There's a book inside all of us," they say. And maybe that's why I wanted to expel from me a book that I'd write if I had the talent, and also the perseverance.

I'm feeling like a mermaid out of water. On one half of me the scales are jewels shining in the sun of life. For I came out of the sea into life. And I wriggle my body atop a large rock combing my long salty hair. I don't know why I wrote that, I think it's so I won't forget to take note of something.

I don't write, for I'm lazy and fluttering. I want to live so much and I think that writing isn't living. That it's enough to feel. I can't do anything for myself in this sense: I've already freed myself from my typewriter and demand to be left to my destiny.

AUTHOR: I don't write because I want to, no. I write because I must. Otherwise what would I do with myself?

Everything I'm being or doing or thinking has a musical accompaniment. There are entire and consecutive days that are accompanied by a powerful and gloomy organ. When I'm being hard on myself the accompaniment is a quartet.

I almost don't know what I feel, if in fact I feel at all. Whatever doesn't exist comes to exist when it receives a name. I write to bring things into existence and to exist myself. Since I was a child I've been searching for the breath of the word that gives life to murmurings. The only reason I never became a real writer is because I get too lost between the lives and my life. And also because I need to put order in my life, in that chaos from which this grave and non-assimilable life is made. I can't relate to my life.

Serious like a boy of 13. Serious like an open mouth singing. The annunciation.

How rude: making me wait.

Seeing is a miracle. How can you describe a pyramid? How can you describe a light turned on?

ANGELA: I'm so ashamed to write. Fortunately I don't publish. When we speak to God we shouldn't use words. The only way to make contact is by being alive and mute, like the needle of a wise and unconscious compass.

AUTHOR: They objectify me when they call me a writer. I never was a writer and never shall be. I refuse to have the role of scribe in the world.

I hate it when they tell me to write or expect me to write. I once received an anonymous letter spiritually offering me a musical recital as long as I kept writing. The result: I stopped completely. Who orders me around—only I know.

ANGELA: I don't write complicated. It's smooth like a gentle sea with waves spreading out white and frigid: agnus-dei.

But does anyone hear me? So I cry out: mama, and I am a daughter and I am a mother. And I have in me the virus of cruel violence and sweetest love. My children: I love you with my poor body and my rich soul. And I swear to tell the truth and nothing but the truth. Entangled in terror. Amen.

In the performance of my obligations I put each thing in its proper place. That's right: the performance of my obligations. To refer to the "discharge" of my obligations would suggest a brown and ugly wound on the leg of a beggar and we feel so guilty about the beggar's wound and its filthy discharge and the beggar is us, the banished.

So delicate and trembling like picking up a station with the portable radio. Even new batteries sometimes refuse. And suddenly it comes in weak or too loud the blessed station I want, weightless as a mosquito. Has anyone ever talked about the dry and brief little noise that the match makes when the ember and orangish flame light up?

I'm waiting for the inspiration for me to live.

I like children so much, I'd love to publish a son named João!

AUTHOR: What this book is missing is a bang. A scandal. A prison. But there will be no prison, and the bang is an implosion.

Angela writes columns for the newspaper. Weekly columns, but she's not satisfied. Columns are not literature, they're sub-literature. Other people might think they're high quality but she considers them mediocre. What she would like is to write a novel but that's impossible because she doesn't have the stamina for it. Her short stories were rejected by the publishers, some of whom said that they were very far from reality. She's going to try to write a story within the "reality" of others, but that would be debasing herself. She doesn't know what to do. Meanwhile her current tapestry goes on: she weaves while her friends are talking. To occupy her hands, she weaves for hours and hours. In her first and only exhibition of tapestries. It seems she's better at weaving than writing columns.

Book of Angela

ANGELA: "Ladies and gentlemen: I am afraid my subject is rather an exciting one and as I don't like excitement, I shall approach it in a gentle, timid, roundabout way"

[MAX BEERBOHM]

"But I love excitement"

[ANGELA PRALINI]

"The only thing that interests me is whatever cannot be thought—whatever can be thought is too little for me"

[ANGELA PRALINI]

AUTHOR: I need to be careful. Angela already senses that she's being driven by me. She must not detect my existence, almost as we can't detect the existence of God.

Angela apparently wants to write a book studying things and objects and their aura. But I doubt she's up to it. Her observations instead of being fashioned into a book arise casually from her way of speaking. Since she likes to write, I write hardly anything about her, I let her speak for herself.

ANGELA: I'd really like to describe still lifes. For example, the three tall and pot-bellied bottles on the marble table: bottles silent as if home alone. Nothing of what I see belongs to me in its essence. And the only use I make of them is to look.

AUTHOR: Needless to say Angela will never write the novel that she puts off every day. She doesn't know that she lacks the capacity to deal with the making of a book. She's inconsistent. All she can do is jot down random phrases. There's only one area in which she, if she really were someone to go through with a vocation, could have some continuity: her interest in discovering the volatile aura of things.

ANGELA: Tomorrow I'll start my novel of things.

AUTHOR: She won't start anything. First of all because Angela never finishes what she starts. Second because her sparse notes for the book are all fragmentary and Angela doesn't know how to bring together and build. She'll never be a writer. That spares her the suffering of barrenness. She's very wise to put herself on the margins of life and enjoy the simple irresponsible commentary. And she by not writing a book escapes what I feel when I finish a book: the poverty of soul, and a draining of the sources of energy. Could it be that anyone says that writing is the work of the lazy?

This book the pseudo-writer Angela is making will be called "Story of Things." (Oneiric suggestions and incursions into the unconscious.)

Angela is someone who sees and studies things in order to use them for sculpture or because she likes sculpture. She's such an autonomous character that she is interested in things that have nothing to do with me, the author. I observe her writing about objects. It's a free-form study in which I take no part. Whereas for Angela things are personal for me the study of the thing is too abstract.

ANGELA: Writing—I tear things out of me in pieces the way a harpoon hooks into a whale and rips its flesh …

AUTHOR: … while I'd like to tear the flesh off words. For each word to be a dry bone under the sun. I am the Day. Only one thing connects me to Angela: we're the human species.

ANGELA: I don't even know how to start. I only know that I'm going to speak of the world of things. I swear that the thing has an aura.

AUTHOR: Everyone who learned to read and write has a certain desire to write. It's legitimate: every being has something to say. But you need more than desire in order to write. Angela says, as thousands of people do (and they're right): "my life is a real novel, if I wrote it down no one would believe me." And it's true. The life of every person is susceptible to a painful deepening and the life of every person is "unbelievable." What should those people do? What Angela does: write with no strings attached. Sometimes writing a single line is enough to save your own heart.

ANGELA: This is a compact book. I beg pardon and permission to pass. There's still no explanation. But one day there will be. The music of this book is "Rhapsody for Clarinet and Orchestra" by Debussy. Trumpets by Darius Milhaud. It's the sexual revelation of what exists. The Wedding March from Wagner's *Lohengrin*. Georges Auric "The Speech of the General." And now—now I'll begin:

—What is nature but the mystery that surrounds everything? Each thing has its place. What the pyramids of Egypt tell us. From the height of such incomprehension, from the top of the pyramid, how many centuries, I contemplate thee, oh ignorance. And I know the secret of the sphinx. She did not devour me because I gave the right answer to her question. But I am an enigma for the sphinx and nevertheless I did not devour her. Decipher me, I said to the sphinx. And she fell mute. The pyramids are eternal. They will always be restored. Is the human soul a thing? Is it eternal? Between the hammer blows I hear the silence.

AUTHOR: Because Angela is such novelty and unusual I get scared. I'm scared in bedazzlement and fear in the face of her impromptu talk. Am I imitating her? or is she imitating me? I don't know: but her way of writing reminds me ferociously of mine as a child can resemble the father. The ancestral fathers. I come from afar. I'm efficient, Angela isn't. I give her some room to move around as though she were a mechanical toy and she sets to work clatteringly. I then remove the clatter oiling her screws and coils. But she doesn't operate under my mechanistic approach: she only acts (through words) when I let her be.

ANGELA: I can't look at an object too much or it sets me on fire. More mysterious than the soul is matter. More enigmatic than the thought, is the "thing." The thing that is miraculously concrete in your hands. Furthermore, the thing is great proof of the spirit. A word is also a thing—a winged thing that I pluck from the air with my mouth when I speak. I make it concrete. The thing is the materialization of aerial energy. I am an object that time and energy gathered in space. The laws of physics govern my spirit and gather in a visible block my body of flesh.

Can paralysis transform a person into a thing? No, it can't, because that thing thinks. I am urgently needing to be born. It's really hurting me. But if I can't get out of this situation, I'll suffocate. I want to scream. I want to scream to the world: I am born!!!

And so I breathe. And so I have the freedom to write about the things of the world. Because it's obvious that the thing is urgently begging for mercy since we abuse it. But if we're in a mechanistic age, we also give our spiritual cry.

The object—the thing—always fascinated me and in a certain sense destroyed me. In my book *The Besieged City* I speak indirectly about the mystery of the thing. The thing is a specialized and immobilized animal. Years ago I also described an armoire. Then came the description of an age-old clock called Sveglia: an electronic clock that haunted me and would haunt any living person. Then it was the telephone's turn. In "The Egg and the Hen" I speak of an industrial crane. It's a timid approach of mine to subverting the living world and the threatening world of the dead.

No, life is not an operetta. It's a tragic opera in which in a fantastic ballet are mingled eggs, clocks, telephones, ice skaters and the portrait of a stranger who died in 1920.

AUTHOR: Angela writes about objects as she would do needlework. A lacemaking woman.

ANGELA: The thing dominates me. But the dog that exists in me barks and there is an outburst of the fatal thing. There is a fatal aspect to my life. I accepted long ago the fearful destiny that is mine. Thank you. Thank you very much, my lord. I'm leaving: I'm going to what is mine. My heart is as cold as the small sound of ice in a glass of whiskey. One day I shall speak of ice. Out of nervousness I broke a glass. And the world exploded. And I broke a mirror. But I didn't look at myself in it. I'm going to investigate things. I hope they won't avenge themselves on me. Forgive me, thing, forgive my pitiful self. Ah what a sigh of the world.

AUTHOR: Angela fell in love with the sight of "things." "Things" for her are an experience almost without the atmosphere of any thought or common expression. However, when she observes things, she acts with a tie that binds her to them. She's not immune. She humanizes things. So she's not honest in her intentions.

ANGELA: When I look, the thing comes to exist. I see the thing in the thing. Transmutation. I sculpt with my eyes anything I see. The thing itself is immaterial. What is called "thing" is the solid and visible condensation of a part of its aura. The aura of the thing is different from the aura of a person. The aura of the latter ebbs and flows, disappears and reappears, turns sweet or flies into a purple rage, explodes and implodes. While the aura of the thing is always the same as itself. The aura distinguishes things. And us too. And the animals that are given the name of a breed and a species. But my own aura trembles glittering when I see you.

AUTHOR: I wanted to write something wide and free. Not to describe Angela but to lodge myself temporarily within her way of being. Angela has but a meager thread of life. And she doesn't insist that anything unusual should happen to her. But I want the intangible thing: the way she makes her way.

To look at the thing in the thing: its intimate meaning as shape, shadow, aura, function. From now on I shall study the profound still life of objects seen with delicate superficiality, and an intentional one, for if it were not superficial it would sink into the past or the future of the thing. I want only the present state of the thing born from nature or the things made by man. This way of feeling is so new to me that it's a revolution. In this my way of looking I see the aura of Angela.

When I look I forget that I am I, I forget I have a face that gets excited and I transform all of myself into a single intense gaze.

Angela when she writes is actually writing about her own aura: I suddenly realized this now. It's no use to nail her down because it's impossible to see her. All you can do is get to the edge of her aura. Despite having a body Angela is intangible —

such are the humidly sparkling mutations of her personality.

I leave you for now to contemplate a dreaming Angela innocently wondering: how will the first springtime be after my death?

ANGELA: The "thing" is properly strictly the "thing." The thing is neither sad nor happy: it is thing. The thing has in itself a plan. The thing is exact. Things make the following noise: chpt! chpt! chpt! A thing is a mangled being. There is nothing more alone than a "thing."

First of all there exists the unity of beings by which each thing is one with itself—it consists of itself, adheres to itself. And so we reach the common conception of the brain as a kind of computer and of human beings as simple autonomous conscious.

AUTHOR: Does Angela have the spontaneity of an initiative or is she just my echo repeated in seven caverns until she dies? Nothing like that. What is it? This: I only hear myself in the repeated echo because my voice initially gets confused with myself.

ANGELA: I entered a silent realm of what is made by the empty hand of man: I entered the domain of the thing. The aura is the sap of the thing. Fluid emanations glaringly blind my vision. I quiver trembling. I tremble quivering. There's something squalid in the air. I breathe it in greedily. I want to fill myself with the physical properties of all that exists in matter. The aura of the thing comes from the reverse of the thing. My reverse side is a splendor of velvety light. I have telepathy with the thing. Our auras overlap. The thing is inside out and the wrong way.

AUTHOR: Angela wants to be fashionable. There's been a lot of talk about "auras." So she writes about it. It's not her fault she's a poor woman with nothing but money. Why doesn't she write about "how can you tell if a mosquito is male or female"?

ANGELA: The spirit of the thing is the aura that surrounds the shapes of its body. It is a halo. It is a breath. It is a breathing. It is a manifestation. It is the freed movement of the thing. I love objects that vibrate in their immobility just as I am a part of the great energy of the world. I have so much energy, that I place static things or those endowed with movement on the same level of energy. I have within me, object that I am, a bit of enigmatic sanctity. I feel it in certain empty moments and I perform miracles within myself: the miracle of the transitory sudden change, at a slight touch in me, to suddenly change feelings and thoughts, and the miracle of seeing everything hollow and clear: I see luminosity without theme, without story, without facts. I make a great effort not to have the worst of feelings: that nothing is worthwhile. And even pleasure is unimportant. So I keep myself busy with things. I've got a problem: it's this: how long do things last? If I leave a sheet of paper in a closed room would it attain eternity? There is a time when things no longer end. Their auras are petrified. If well taken care of, a piece of paper will never end. Or is it transformed?

I ask you in what realm you were last night. And the answer is: I was in the realm of whatever is free, I breathed in the grand solitude of the dark and leaned over the edge of the moon. The late night made such silence. Just like the silence of an object placed upon a table: aseptic silence of "the thing." There also exists great silence in the sound of a flute: it unwinds vast distances of hollow spaces of black silence until the end of time.

AUTHOR: I don't want to violate the soul of Angela and break it into loose words without any intimate connection: but how do I approach her without invading her? how to make a speech out of something that's no more than scream or sweetness or nothing or craziness or vague ideal? Could it be I have to use her in order to reveal a more inconsistent mode that I too have within me? I who besides a desire for method, want laughter or weeping like quick summer showers. One proof that I misuse Angela's scant life is that she writes with a style that's actually my own. The truth is that I'm going to take advantage of Angela's kind of audacity to venture a little madness but with the guarantee of "returning."

ANGELA: *"Woman-Thing."*

I'm the unworked raw material. I'm also an object. I have all the necessary organs, like any human being. I feel my aura which on this chilly morning is red and extremely sparkly. I am a woman object and my aura is a vibrant and competent red. I am an object that sees other objects. Some are brothers to me and others are enemies. There are also objects that say nothing. I am an object that uses other objects, that enjoys or rejects them.

My face is an object so visible it's embarrassing. I understand those beautiful Arab women who have the wisdom to hide their noses and mouths with a veil or white crêpe. Or purple. So all that is exposed are the eyes that reflect other objects. The gaze then gains such a terrible mystery that it looks like the vortex of an abyss. I use scarlet-red lipstick: that's my provocation. I've got eyebrows that are always asking but don't argue, they are delicate. This face-object has a small and rounded nose that allows the object that I am to sniff around like a hunting dog. I have some secrets: my eyes are such a dark green that they seem black. In photographs of this face of which I speak to you with a certain solemnity my eyes refuse to be green: a strange face appears in the photograph with black and slightly Oriental eyes.

One object thinks of another object and our auras get confused. And I have, I assure you, everything else that makes me a woman sometimes living, sometimes object. My essential stupidity however wants to tremble with light, to be glorified by spirit. My heaviness needs the adventure of hazarding guesses. This being who calls me to light, how I shall bless him! I shall open myself to him in my stupidity which is a granite block.

Bells of gold are ringing in me sacred bells. And my purple drapes have been ready. The color purple is abysmal and has no end. Its noble intensity. I keep looking and going deeper into the endlessness of the old clot as when I try to perforate dense matter with my eyes. Purple leaves me pensive dreaming and empty.

AUTHOR: Angela is obsessed with giving names to things. She doesn't know how to simply feel them without thinking.

What would become of me if not for Angela? the woman enigma who makes me emerge from the nothing and head toward the word.

ANGELA: *"Mother-Thing."*

I opened myself and you from me were born. One day I opened myself and you were born for you yourself. How much gold poured out. And how much rich blood was spilled. But it was all worth it: you are the pearl of my heart that is shaped like a bell of pure silver. I dissipated. And you were born. And I erased myself so you could have the freedom of a god. You are pagan but have the blessing of a mother.

And. And the mother is me.

A swollen mother. Mother sap. Mother tree. Mother who gives and asks nothing in return.

Mother organ music.

Raise the flag, son, at the hour of my holy death. And I give such a profound cry of horror and praise that things shatter at the vibration of my only voice. Collision of stars. Through the enormous monstrous telescope you see me. And I am icy and generous as the sea. I die. And I come from afar like the silent Ravel. I am a portrait watching you. But when you wish to be alone with your girlfriend-wife cover my sweet face with a dark and opaque cloth—and I shall see nothing. I am mother-thing hanging from the wall with respect and sorrow. But what deep happiness there is in being a mother. A mother is crazy. So crazy that from her children are born. I nourish myself with rich foods and you suck from me thick and phosphorescent milk. I am your talisman.

AUTHOR: Angela, control yourself so as not to write a tear-jerker about a poor boy with his mother dead.

ANGELA: *"Folding Screen."*

My folding screen is made of round cylinders of jacaranda. I'd almost say that jacaranda is sterling silver. As there is a small gap between one cylinder and the next it remains open to consequences. And its fragility is dangerous. Because when it falls—and it falls at the slightest push—it smashes the plants behind it. My screen is my way of looking at the world! between-the-slats.

AUTHOR: In this talking of mine and of Angela's, we both transcend the bourgeoisie inside us. What drives me to despair is the fact-idea that Angela is ambiguous in her existence: part of her is independent, another part is the wife selected by me like a chosen daughter.

Well, but with this book I, it seems I'm emancipating myself. Which is good and about time. This almost emancipation also leaves me standing and alone in the world. I don't have anything to nourish me: I eat myself.

ANGELA: *"State of the Thing."*

The desert is a way of being. It's a thing-state. By day it's torrid and devoid of pity. It's the thing-earth. The dry thing in thousands and thousands of trillions of grains of sand. By night? So cold that sheet of air that furrows trembling with such an intense cold of an intensity almost unbearable. The color of the desert is not-a-color. The sands are not white, they are the color of dirtiness. And the dunes, which like echoes undulate feminine. By day the air sparkles. And there are mirages. You see—because you so want to see it—an oasis of humid and fertile earth, palms and water, shade, shade at last for eyes that in the mad sun become emerald-green. But when you get close—well: it simply never was. It was no more than a creation of the sun in the uncovered head. The body takes pity on the body. I am a mirage: because I so long to see myself I do.

Ah, the dunes of the desert of the Sahara seem long asleep, untransformable by the passing of days and of nights. If its sands were white or colored, they would have "facts" and "events," which would shorten time. But with the color they are, nothing happens. And when it does, a rigid, immobile, thick, swollen, thorny, bristling, intractable cactus happens. The cactus is full of rage with fingers all twisted and it's impossible to caress it: it hates you with each piercing spine because it also feels the pain of the spine that pierced its own thick flesh first. But you can cut it into pieces and suck its bitter sap: the milk of a stern mother. To soften this life of mine that slowly drips drop upon drop—I have the power of the mirage: I see humid oases that vanish when I approach seeking maternal shelter. A hard life is a life that seems longer. But, even so, what surprises me is how it can already be May, if only yesterday it was February? Each minute that comes is a miracle that cannot be repeated.

AUTHOR: I don't have a single answer. But I have more questions than any man could answer.

ANGELA: The phrase "damp garden" gives me a gentle happiness and a canticle spreading from me to me. The words "drinking-well" and "pergola" also make me wet. Ah could I but describe the delicate happiness they inspire in me, only then would I be a writer. I'd be dizzy with pleasure.

AUTHOR: Angela doesn't write. She moans.

ANGELA: I wanted to write luxuriously. To use words that would shine wet and glistening and were pilgrims. Sometimes solemn in purple, sometimes abysmal emeralds, sometimes so light in the finest soft embroidered silk. I wanted to write random phrases, phrases that would go beyond speaking back to me: "the morning moon," "gardens and gardens in shade," "astringent sweetnesses of honey," "crystals that break with a musical disastrous crash." Or to use words that come to me from my unknown: trapilíssima avante sine qua non masioty—poor us and you. You are my lit candle. I am the Night.

AUTHOR: What I'm writing is an intense and basic work, foolish like certain experiences that don't collaborate with the future and are therefore useless. What Angela writes is of an essential superfluousness because her life even if superfluous follows a freedom to and fro: while I Angela is always now. One now follows another now and etc. and so on.

ANGELA: *"The Indescribable"*

I bought a thing with which I fell absolutely in love: the price doesn't matter, this object is worth the very air.

This thing has a solid base of metal, very concise. In this shining cylinder there is the slightest opening. In it you put delicate and slender metal stems. And atop each stem there sits in glory a tiny and round ball that looks like a jewel of sterling silver.

This object is magical. A breath or a light touch of the hand is enough—and it vibrates all over intermingling sparklingly with the air. Is it an object of the moon or of the sun? it's like good news, like being happily startled, like a "suddenly." It has thirty little balls and stems. But it's deceiving: when they start to vibrate and move they're like a delicate trillion little balls. There's one more thing it has: when the lights in the room come on, the little balls cast a shadow, greenish.

And there's more: when it vibrates as a result of the slight shock of the balls against each other—some musical notes result. And the object if well made and induced sings swiftly—a swift Do Re Mi …

"Grabbing the word." I grab the word and make it thing.

I grabbed joy and made it like a brilliant crystal in the air. Joy is a crystal. Nothing needs to have shape. But the thing absolutely must in order to exist.

"Silver Box"

Has it ever occurred to you to feel sorry for an object? I have a medium-sized silver box and it inspires pity in me. I don't know what in this silent, immobile object makes me understand its solitude and the punishment of eternity. I don't place any-thing inside the box so that it won't be burdened.

And the heavy lid encloses the void. I always place flow-ers around it so they can relieve the life-death of the box—the flowers are also an homage to the anonymous artisan who sculpted in heavy sterling silver a work of art.

"The House"

This is a castle of solid stone. But its aura is a nest of soft moonlight. Upon it the sun shines like a mirror.

The greatest thing one can have is the house. Beethoven understood this and composed a resplendent symphonic over-ture called "The Consecration of the House." I heard this mu-sic that reassures me at six-thirty on a still sleepy morning. Hearing such remarkable music provoked a delirious dream in which the things of the house moved around and were be-witched. So I thought: I must simply must have enormous corollas of fine smooth but wild feathers to place in my house.

I looked at the stone upon the table. It was large and very heavy. I plunged into vague meditation. I looked at it. Almost black. And inexorable.

One way of living more is to use your senses in a context not properly their own. For example: I see a marble table that is naturally to be seen. But I stroke as subtly as possible its form, I feel its coldness, I imagine the scent of "thing" the marble must have, scent that for us exceeds the smell barrier and we can't feel it through our noses, we can only imagine it.

The teapot so slender, elegant and full of grace. Yes, but all this passes in an instant, and what is left is an old and slightly chipped teapot, ordinary object.

Author: I don't know what the climax of this book will be. But, as Angela goes on writing, I'll recognize it.

Angela: "*The Clock*"

You feel in the clock time vibrating. Meanwhile, that is, while I look at the hours of the clock life is evaporating and my heart becomes an object that sparkles. If I were God I would see man, at a distance, as thing. We are of divine construction.

The clock is a torturing object: it seems shackled to time. The second hand, if we kept watching it move mechanically and inexorably, would put us in a frenzy.

"*Iron Guardrail*"

Bad weather.

I, deteriorated.

At the back of the courtyard I saw an iron guardrail in a sorry state, all corroded and peeling with rust. I lingered staring at it, without getting any closer. I didn't know why I was staring at it with such concentration. And suddenly it seemed that the guardrail was looking at me. It was tall and rose with an intensity of thing. I felt consecrated. Afterwards I gave a deep sigh with my eyes shut, and I opened them again as if I had been sleeping and finally awoke, forgetting my dream, I awoke arriving from very far within myself. I breathed deeply and looked once again at the slender rail. And as I looked I saw that that haughty thing was nothing, it wasn't looking at me, and would cross another century.

Author: The process that Angela has for writing is the same process as the act of dreaming: what starts forming are images, colors, acts, and especially an atmosphere of dreams that resembles a color and not a word. She doesn't know how to explain herself. All she knows is how to do and to do without understanding herself.

ANGELA: *"The Car"*
    The photographer Francis Giacobetti, of the magazine *Lui*, spends all of his working hours taking nude portraits of the most beautiful girls in and around Paris.
    He was asked, in an article about nudes published in the latest *L'Express*, what he most liked photographing, above all else? "Not women, no. Trucks. They're beautiful, trucks ..."
    The red scream.
    The scarlet-red car let out a purple howl. That "thing" had a horn. And it screamed calling the attention of passers-by. And of God. That "thing" has coils, it has rubber, it has a radio.

AUTHOR: Angela sometimes writes phrases that have absolutely nothing to do with what she'd been discussing. I think these unexpected interferences are like electric static that interferes and gets mixed up with the music on the radio. The electrical currents in the air simply stick to her. And if that happens it's because she doesn't know how to write, she writes everything, without selecting. I myself, if I'm not careful, sometimes pick up some electrical interference and suddenly start talking about an orange tractor. The tractor comes to mind because I'm unintentionally plagiarizing Angela.

ANGELA: Example of a phrase that's enigmatic and completely hermetic like a closed thing: "calibrating tires." Those words delight and seduce me. To calibrate is to give caliber, isn't it? Yes. So when I see a sign on a truck reading: "Inflammable"—then I am filled with glory.

A mobile crane mounted on a Scania-Vabis chassis and with an 18–22 ton capacity. It's the "Iron Giraffe," originally called "Hudra Truck 18/22-T and which is being manufactured in Brazil. Initially, the production schedule estimates three monthly units increasing to five, next year, with great export possibilities."

And so I see that the crane will have children and one day will populate the earth. Which will be a world of objects. But the objects no longer want to be objects. It's the revolt of the "thing." The catastrophe of things is a noisy racket in the air. Only for the supersonic.

AUTHOR: A fatal mechanization makes Angela see "things" more and not human beings.

ANGELA: "*Record Player*"

On the record the black circumvolutions avoid mixing with other magic circles by a hair: and from there comes the aura of music. I have a musical aura. The record I pick it up and run the hairs of my arm across and the hairs stand on end. Because its aura touches mine.

"*Butterfly*"

The mechanics of the butterfly. First it's the egg. Later the egg breaks and a caterpillar comes out. This caterpillar is hermetically sealed. It isolates itself atop a leaf. Inside it is a cocoon. But the caterpillar is opaque. Until it starts turning transparent. Its aura shines, it fills with colors. Then from the caterpillar that opens itself there emerge small fragile legs. At that the entire butterfly comes out. Then the butterfly slowly opens its wings above the leaf—and takes off fluttering, light, happy, a little crazy. Its life is brief but intense. Its mechanics are higher mathematics.

I saw a black butterfly. It cursed me.

AUTHOR: She turns a butterfly into an epic. And she's unorthodox.

ANGELA: Living is almost intolerable.

I see death smiling in your beautiful face like the fatal stain of the face of Christ on Veronica's veil.

If we could stay quiet—suddenly an egg is born. An alchemical egg. And I'm being born and I'm breaking the dry shell of the egg with my lovely beak. I'm born! I'm born! I'm born!

My soul is racked by desire.

Oh scarlet eggplant, what are you? are you a thing? bitter as life itself. I'm going to try everything I can, I don't want to keep distant from the world.

AUTHOR: Angela—if she really could write—would give us her rough ideas because she's incapable of addressing a possible reader with the spontaneous lack of order she uses to write this book. She thinks that contact with the reader can only happen through complicated reasoning.

ANGELA: *"Trash Can"*

The trash can is a luxury. Because who doesn't have things to put out in the street the things that aren't any use? and yet we have a container made just for our rubbish. If we threw our trash onto the street it would become a federal problem. Scrap metal is the most beautiful garbage there is.

"I'm clean and don't smell. But as fate would have it they fill me with filth and dirt. Only mutts understand me. 'She' lines me with newspaper: *Jornal do Brasil*. And I unafraid pretend I have no owner. I receive stubbed-out butts of cigarettes. One day I'll catch fire. At night I'm alone in the dark, empty, left in the corner on the ground. My silence stinks. Woe is me, receptacle of the death of things."

The number is itself.

The flower is from May 14th.

Numbers ... are they what's hidden behind your mysteries, secret effluvia and succulent secretions or, maybe, sibilant and pointed questions without any answers? What do they hide, clouds?

As for the sea. The sea is impossible to believe. Only by imagining it can you manage to see its reality. Only as a possible dream does the sea exist. But the bottomlessness of the sea blossoms inside me with the scare of a scarecrow.

A vase with pale roses already wilting is a phantasmagoric thing that profoundly frightens me when it catches me unawares. They threaten to throw into the air their own aura that becomes a ghost.

And the picture of painted roses gives a smile. I'm afraid of living roses because they are so fragile and dandyish and because they turn yellow. But painted roses they don't frighten me.

To be alone is a state of being. I learned this from things. It's obvious, it's clear that things tend to be alone. But a living room set is so lonely!

The armchair is mute, it's fat, it's cozy. It greets every backside like any other. It's a mother. On the other hand the edge of a table is a fateful weapon. If you were thrown against it, you'd double over in pain. A round table is sly. But it presents no danger: it's a bit mysterious, it smiles slightly.

AUTHOR: Angela has an enviable quality: she's chatty when she describes "things," she seems to bear good news.

ANGELA: You shouldn't live in luxury. In luxury we become an object that in turn possesses other objects. You only see the "thing" when you live a monastic life or at least a temperate life. The spirit can live on bread and water.

The violin mute thing exhales restrained music but with sleeping eyes. A violin that reaches the paroxysm of piercing sound: the glory of being.

Matchsticks flare restless inside the sealed box, mad for the sexual act that consists of being struck on the black part of the box and transforming into fire. Yet the match does not know that it will catch and burn but a single time.

"The Jewel"

It shines. This it without equal. It is always unique. And has sacred rage.

But when it's a pearl necklace it shines softly like the piety of an Ave Maria. A pearl necklace needs to be in contact with our skin in order to receive our heat. Otherwise it dies. One, two, three, seven, how many pearly eggs of mother-of-pearl? And it ends with the most delicate clasp of diamonds set in white gold.

White gold? it turns pale in terror: threat.

Whereas sun-gold gives itself openly like a glory of love. A long gold chain runs through the fingers like warm water of a brook between sunlit pebbles. Sun-gold doesn't refuse. But— but, my God, how dangerous is the gold ingot. Men kill for a yellow brick.

A woman sells herself for a diamond. And a greedy one asks for more: she wants a very wide stole of warm mink.

Brilliants are small joys in a shower of children's laughter. They're cold little waterfalls in bursts of trembling giggles. Oh how cold. I prefer the word brilliants to diamonds. I'm not sure why: maybe because the word "brilliant" actually seems to shine brilliantly with its flashes of diagonal light, it's a word that seems not to consist only of itself, of a single brilliant, but to contain a shower of brilliants, like illuminated and transparent eyes. Brilliants are a joy of the earth, they jump about and when still seem like stars. In fact, brilliants are never still: their crystalline light is refractory to immobility. A brilliant lights up any setting and one's eyes become gently cleared. But a diamond is something chained to the earth, it's solid, and the word "diamante," "diamond," is a bit opaque despite its first two syllables: "dia," "day." And the end "amante," "lover," reveals a carnal and imperishable love. The brilliant is poetically irresponsible, whereas the diamond-stone is circumspect and stable.

But a brooch is serious. It's an argument. It leaps into the air like a woman-gazelle. It fastens, it's weighty, it waits. And when unfastened—everything becomes naked, the curtain falls and the white breasts seem to blush. The brooch is a period.

Exclamations are the dangling earrings that tremble between strands of hair. An earring made of what? made of everything that knows how extremely important it is to shine. Earrings are extremelies. And the earring of a single and modest pearl is the violet of jewels. But diamond earrings fight and utter small cries that frighten me. They quarrel, cruel. An earring of sterling silver is seriousness and a guarantee of great and strict security. A gold earring is any old "this," it's a little this without much importance. Unless it's a round ball of gold: then it's possession and activity.

Instantaneous is the light and brief ring of pearls. And when there are many pearls on the ring—they are a smile and an ellipsis. Between parentheses is the ring of diamonds set in white gold because in secret it says an "I-love-you" in Greek.

AUTHOR: I realize with surprise but with resignation that Angela is controlling me. She even writes better than I do. Now our ways of speaking are intersecting and getting confused.

ANGELA: Wild coral is jagged and the isle of Capri in the sun. A coral necklace cannot be grabbed by the hand: it wounds the delicate shell of that white and nervous hand.

Around the neck, the coral necklace is Christ's crown of thorns.

Ah! The diadem! I am the queen! I blaze like the high crown that I am. Kings use me in the shape of a papal triangular hood. Young princesses adorn with delicate diadems their fresh and innocent faces that are yet capable of cruelty. Marie Antoinette crowned and lovely, months before her head was chopped off and rolled in the street, cried out melodiously: if the people have no bread, let them eat cake. And the response was: allons enfants de la patrie, le jour de gloire est arrivé. The people devoured what they could and ate jewels and ate trash and guffawed. Meanwhile the pale face of Marie Antoinette displayed pearly silence on a head without hair and without a neck.

Jade grants me divinity. Its traversable green sanctifies me as a Byzantine icon. I, hands clasped together before my serious and transparent face and my diadem are then the entwined braids of my vigorous and tranquil strands of black hair. Jade is my sword unsheathed for the hara-kiri of my humble proud soul that kills itself because it has so little of everything, it's poverty-stricken, but it has the sovereign pride of death.

But—but only the diamond cuts glass.

And now I'm going to say something very serious, pay attention: a shard of glass is a rare jewel. And its shattering is a sound to be heard on bended knee like the tolling of bells. Elegant bells that are jewel things too. Bells are the jewels of the church. And the clapper of the bell is a ringing of gold that shatters in the air in diamonds and blue birds.

A fiery horse is the ruby in which I plunge so deep that I tear myself apart.

And the emerald? The emerald is something to gnaw with your teeth, and shatter into a thousand little shards of small green children of emeralds.

Topaz is the transparency of your gaze.

The stone? the stone on the ground? It's a jewel that came from the sky in a whirlwind and stopped right there until I came and saw it and grabbed it and felt it like something of my own, something of my heart.

And the sapphire? it has a reflection that blinds the eyes of the reckless who buy sapphires as if they were diamonds. I've never seen a sapphire. I only know what I've heard. But the day I come face-to-face with a sapphire—ah! it'll be sword against sword and we'll see if I'll be the one from whom the blood will gush.

The bracelet enslaves me, oh sweet enslavement of a woman to her favorite man.

Platinum is the most expensive. But I don't want you, you're ferocious in your white iciness. I prefer the cheap jewelry of a poor woman who buys in the public market diamonds taken from the purest water of the murky sewers.

Amethyst, I do not kiss you because I am not your servant.

Onyx! black prince of roses, you make me bitter and I swim in the waters—darkness of your iron grip, oh mourning of a queen! downy black spider. May you be cursed, black stone of blood, clot of humors and miasmas.

Aquamarine? when I was a child my first boyfriend had blue aquamarine eyes. But I didn't get close to him: I was afraid. Because still waters run deep and gave me chills.

Jewel

Frisson

Betrayal

But profound regret

And me, just me, resting alert inside the jewel-box of purple velvet.

AUTHOR: Angela—of course—has a conscious mind that doesn't get along well with her subconscious. Is she double? and is her life double? Like this: on the one hand there's the attraction to intellectualized things, on the other, something that seeks the comforting and mysterious and free darkness, unafraid of danger.

ANGELA: *"Elevator"*

My elevator suddenly refused to elevate or lower me. It was simply moving between floors, opening the door automatically and presenting me with the slap in the face of a wall. For days: sulky, angry, vindictive. Pointless because no one wished it ill. We were only using its energy. But it got irritated and decided to be rude. It needed a lot of oil and a lot of back-and-forth to finally make up with us and lower and elevate us.

What I can't tolerate is fuss. The object is mute, it's without any fuss.

There was a gaze of the atmosphere of the room upon me. I felt that gaze like a mysterious comfort.

As for how the rotation of the stars produces the inertia of my ashtray—explain it if you can.

AUTHOR: Angela sometimes nauseates me like a chocolate ice-cream soda.

ANGELA: The retch of perplexity.
    The sky is concentrated air. It's the void.
    Rotten wood.
    Careful, Nature thinks.

AUTHOR: Careful with what? and what does she mean Nature thinks? She's out of her mind.

ANGELA: If you think we're made of wax you're gonna pay.

AUTHOR: For those who write, an idea without words is not an idea. Angela is full of pre-words and unconscious auditory visions of ideas. My job is to cut out her drivel and leave behind only what she at least manages to stammer.

ANGELA: Man sits. Why? Is sitting down something we've acquired slowly through process across millennia? Or is it part of human nature? As it's in a bird's nature to fly? Lying down is different: except for feathered creatures, every animal lies down.

    I sometimes feel such pity for "things." That small table with the marble top, poor thing so cold and white and pale and proud in vain. It thinks it's noble. And my trash basket full of paper, so elegant and simple, woven from strips of wood but what's the point of its beauty if it's always on the floor, always full of the crumpled paper of the letters I didn't send.

Farewell, oh thing.

I'm leaving for when-hell-freezes-over.

AUTHOR: Angela lacks the creative ambition that is made of a hunger that is never satisfied.

Discovering a new way to live. I believe that the key lies in seeing the thing in the thing, without going beyond or behind it, outside its context. The result of such a new way of looking at the passing moment is often to wonder at a thing as if we were seeing it for the first time. Seeing the thing in the thing hypnotizes the person looking at the dazzling object seen. There is an encounter between me and that thing vibrating in the air. But the result of that gaze is a sensation of hollowness, empty, impenetrable and of full mutual recognition. God forgive me I believe I'm rambling on about the nothing. But I'm sure of one thing, this nothing is the best character in a novel. In the void of the nothing facts and things insert themselves. What you see in this way of transforming everything absolutely into the present state, the result is not mental: it is a mute form of feeling absolutely untranslatable by words.

I'm only going to reread superficially what I've already written and what Angela wrote because I don't want to influence myself, I don't want to copy. I don't want to imitate even the truth. Perhaps by reading only superficially what's already been written will I lose the thread and everything will come out fragmentary and disconnected. Or maybe it's disconnected because I speak of one thing that belongs to my path, while Angela speaks of another thing that belongs to her destiny. But, though I am fragmentary and dissonant and out of tune, I believe there exists in all this a hidden order. And! There exists a will.

AUTHOR: I'm in love with a character I invented: Angela Pralini. Here she is speaking:

ANGELA: Ah how I would like a languid life.
   I am one of the interpreters of God.

AUTHOR: When Angela thinks of God, is she referring to God or to me?

ANGELA: Who makes my life? I feel that someone is ordering me around and fating me. As if someone were creating me. But I am also free and don't obey orders.

AUTHOR: I've been drinking too much. When you drink, you end up with a naked subconscious and can only feel, feel, feel. God is a thing you breathe. I don't have faith in God. Luck is sometimes not having faith. Because that way one day you can have The Great Surprise of those who don't expect miracles. It seems moreover that miracles happen like manna from heaven especially for those who believe in nothing. And those people don't even realize that they were singled out. I've grown tired of asking. For the miracle to happen you have to not expect it. I want nothing more.

I am the night and He is the firefly.

The theme of my life is the nothing.

Reality is very strange, it's entirely unreal. Why hast thou forsaken me, my God? I live my life apologizing and giving thanks.

Angela gave God the power to cure her soul. It's a God of great utility: for when Angela feels God then the terribly exposed truth is immediate. Angela uses God to breathe. She divides God to use Him as her protection. Angela is not a mystic and doesn't even see the golden light in the air.

ANGELA: I wanted to lead an ascetic life, of purification, of exclusive contact with the beyond. But how? If at the same time I want money for my comforts, I want a man for my sensuality, I want the precious stones that are the gem of the earth and that are for that reason also sacred? My duality surprises me, I'm dizzy and unhappy. At the same time it's a richness to have the element sky-air and the element earth-love, without one getting in the way of the other.

The moment I grasp myself—I shall have reached eternity no matter how ephemeral.

God was not made for us. We are the ones who were made for Him. What we must do, though He doesn't care for us, is adore Him and in the worst circumstances fill our hearts with the pleasure of praising Him.

AUTHOR: A man imagined God and made a chair, in that chair there must be a bit of that man's energy. Such is the spirit of made things, lived things.

I invented God—and don't believe in Him. It's as if I had written a poem about the nothing and then suddenly found myself face-to-face with the nothing itself. Is God a word? If so then I'm full of Him: thousands of words crammed inside a jar that's shut and that I sometimes open—and I am dazzled. God-word is dazzling.

ANGELA: Sometimes, just to feel myself living, I think about death. Death justifies me.

An object ages because it has within it dynamics.

Instead of saying "my world," I say audaciously: the world depends on me. Because if I don't exist, the Universe ceases within me. Could it be that abstraction begins after death?

I, reduced to a word? but what word represents me? I know one thing: I am not my name. My name belongs to those who call me. But, my intimate name is: zero. It is an eternal beginning permanently interrupted by my awareness of beginning.

God is neither the beginning nor the end. He is always the middle.

AUTHOR: I participate in Angela's shaking restlessness but do not imitate her.

ANGELA: I'm weak, dubious, there's a charlatan inside me though I tell the truth. And I feel guilty about everything. I who have crises of rage, "sacred rage." And I can't find the refuge of peace. For pity's sake, let me live! I ask for little, it's almost nothing but it's everything! peace, peace, peace! No, my God, I don't want peace with an exclamation mark. I want only this minimum: peace. Just so, very, very slowly … like this … almost asleep … that's right … that's right … it's almost coming … Don't frighten me, I am terribly frightened.

He is the well-applied word. And I rolling through space like a baby without gravity. Where's my gravity? Or are you supposed to say gravitation? Do me a favor, give me somewhere to land. I'm not someone to believe in. But to imagine without managing to. It makes me want to talk wrong. Like: Dog. That means God.

AUTHOR: Angela doesn't know how to live gradually: she wants to eat life all at once. And so she's got empty *time* left over. The meditation inside the emptiness is what she manages, being at the last human stage before our lives that are without exception glorious.

Solitary eagle.

Living is a hobby for her. She thinks it has nothing to do with her and lives tossed to the side, without past or future; just today forever.

ANGELA: Is what's happening to me Grace? Because my body I don't feel it, it doesn't weigh me down, it doesn't desire, the spirit neither strains nor searches, a luminous aura of silence envelops me: I hover in the air, free of time but fully in this very moment, without before or after. I greet myself and the world does not touch me. For me to be two and for there to be the participation of this state, I look at myself in the mirror, I look at the other of me. And I see that my fluid appearance has the loveliness of the floating human face. Then I feel with a most delicate pleasure that I'm whole. And an air of truth. I am finally barefoot.

I did what was most urgent: a prayer.

I pray to find my true path. But I discovered that I don't give myself entirely to the *prayer*, I seem to know that the true path is with pain. There is a secret and to me incomprehensible law:

only through suffering does one find happiness. I fear myself because I'm always ready to be able to suffer. If I don't love myself I'll be lost—because no one loves me to the point of being I, of being me. I must want myself in order to give something to myself. Must I be worth something? Oh protect me from myself, who persecutes me. I'm worth something in relation to others—but in relation to myself, I am nothing.

It's so good to have someone to ask for things. It doesn't even bother me much if my requests aren't totally satisfied. I ask God to make me prettier—and isn't it true that my eye shines as my lips seem fuller and sweeter? I ask God for everything I want and need. That's what I can do. Whether my prayers are answered—that's not up to me, that's already the matter-magic that either gives itself to me or withholds itself. Stubborn, I pray. I don't have the power. I have the prayer.

AUTHOR: I'm so in contact with God that I don't even need to pray. It's natural that Angela resembles me a bit. I've even infected her with the mysterious belief I have.

I am afraid to be who I am.

There is a total silence within me. I get scared. How to explain that this silence is what I call the Unknown. I'm afraid of It. Not because It could childishly punish me (punishment is something people do). The fear comes from what surpasses me. And that also is me. Because my greatness is great.

I don't live dangerously in facts. I live in extreme danger when alone I fall into deep meditation. That is when I dangerously become free even of God. And free even of me. At the edge of a precipice dumbstruck on the dry height of a cliff. And as a living thing beside me—only the cactus with its crown of thorns of a nature that forsook me. I am alone from myself.

I constantly got lost inside me. I need the patience of a saint. I am a man who chose silence. I had to love a pure being.

Ah, melancholy of having been created. I'd rather have stayed in the immanescence of nature. Ah, divine wisdom that makes me move without knowing what legs are for.

Does God know He exists?

I think God doesn't know He exists. I'm almost certain He doesn't. And hence His powerful strength.

I cried a lot today and my eyes got swollen and red. But it was worth it. I don't even wonder why I cried.

The worst part is that I'm vice versa and zigzag. I'm inconclusive. But I have to love myself the way I involuntarily am. I only take responsibility for what's voluntary in me and that is very little.

I do not understand, therefore I believe. I believe "in what."

Do you know what God is? God is time. I'm barely a part of this itinerary heading toward Nothing. I wonder with an already rather morbid insistence why was I born. I swear it's not worth the bother for anyone to be me. As for Angela, she keeps up with fashion. For example: people talk a lot these days about "human condition," "existence," "aura." Why the devil doesn't she instead of wanting to dominate objects dedicate herself to figuring out if an insect is male or female? Women have that problem, keeping up with fashion. I don't know what the fashion is now but I know it's time for sex and violence. I myself only watch horror films. There's a cold war that's finishing me off.

Time is the indefinable. I quickly put myself in time, before dying. Life is very quick, when you see it, you've reached the end. And to top it off we're required to love God.

There's a narrow passage inside me, so narrow its walls wound me all over, but that passage leads to the breadth of God. I don't always have the strength to cross this bloody

desert, even knowing that, if I force myself to hurt all over between the walls, even knowing that I'll come out into the open
light of a day trembling with gentle sunshine.

ANGELA: I went trembling to encounter myself—and found
a silly woman flailing between the walls of existence. I smash
the floodgates and create myself anew. And then I can meet I,
on equal footing.
  Did I consecrate myself to God?

AUTHOR: I, vigilant as a lit candle. Watching over the mysteries of Angela.
  Angela doesn't know how to define. That's why for her the
world is much vaster than mine. Not that I know how to define but I'm aware of the limits and limiting yourself makes a
possible definition easier.
  Angela has a gift that I find very moving: the gift of error.
Her whole life is a big mistake. The way she realizes that something inside her is wrong, and very gravely wrong is her anxiety,
her permanent suspicion. She lives askance. Another way she
feels that there's a fundamental error in her life is through her
humility and her innocence. The wicked are the ones who must
be forgiven. The innocent have forgiveness within themselves.
  I do not approve of myself because I can hardly stand to live
with myself. I do almost the impossible to be exempt. Exempt
from myself. I'm almost reaching that state of blessedness.

ANGELA: Today I bought a long dress with tones of emerald-
green, scarlet-red, loud-white, severe-black, king-blue, insane-
yellow.
  God is like listening to music: He fills the being.

Author: She doesn't seem to have what one might call "elevated feelings." She's selfish and covetous. She won't let anyone go partly out of love, partly because she doesn't know how to break things off—but partly because of the nearly luxurious material comfort people give her. She's happy in the diamonds she receives from time to time.

She's not immobile: her active imperfections give her great mobility. It's in sin itself that Angela encounters her God. She's frivolous. Everything she touches turns frivolous. But when I tell her that, she answers with a text she copied from *Reader's Digest*: "Joseph Haydn, criticized for the lightness of his music, smiled: I cannot make it otherwise; I write according to the thoughts I feel. When I think upon God, my heart is so full of joy that the notes dance and leap, as it were, from my pen; and since God has given me a cheerful heart, it will be pardoned me that I serve Him with a cheerful spirit."

I've discovered why I breathed life into Angela's flesh, it was to have someone to hate. I hate her. She represents my terrible faith that is reborn every single morning. And it's frustrating to have faith. I hate this creature who simply seems to believe. I'm sick of her empty God that she fills up with nervous ecstasies. When did the hate in me start to happen and live? And I get all dizzy with the effluvia of a sentiment I ignored in myself for as long as I can remember.

Could it be that I want Angela Pralini in order to develop a feeling that is ardent and sleepless, the feeling of hatred I now need to exercise because she taught me to hate? Are we forever attached? I want her. I know that one day I'll leave her, but my fear is that I won't forget her and shall ever bear that dark stain on my soul. This soul that's always surprised by the novelty of feeling.

For I bathe entirely in that devouring darkness, I want to know the depth of my hatred. I want to know every feeling. Must a person have experienced this cursed power in order to be a complete person? I don't know, but it's demonic.

I'm making a shameful confession: it's good to hate her. My soul, a potential murderer, knows therefore the rich darknesses of blood, and what I know makes me feel the worst of myself. And, yes, the murderous soul is rich. I sometimes wonder if she wants me to kill her to bring me to the summit of my hatred. It's better to forget her because otherwise my own blood begins to hurt me and I'll be filled with a black revolt without at least knowing what I'm revolting against, that's a lie I know quite well what I'm revolting against. But it's something that can't be said.

I get tense thinking of the kind of relaxation in which Angela lives. I can't reach her—now she escapes me, now she's close at hand—and when I think she's within my reach, she rebels, intrinsic.

Time is not measurable.

Angela makes no plans. And she scares herself because she's always a novelty. Sometimes she takes refuge in an impenetrable nest. For example: just now I lost sight of her and don't know where she lives (hidden within me in a dark corner of mine?). And I no longer know what she's going to say. I trust in her unpredictable drive.

Angela Pralini is sometimes unfettered and slightly sharp like the voices of singing boys performing Bach cantatas, or a chorus of monks. Angela is my vocal exercise.

Angela, I don't know how to tell you and begin, without hurting you. But I can't stand you anymore. I'm going to invent another woman quickly. One who won't be magical like you, one in whom I can go about walking the earth and eating meat. I want a real woman. I'm tired of lying.

I'm going to invent a whole woman, who's organized and logical, who has a propensity like that of a surgeon. Or even a lawyer. And who in bed is limpid and without sin. I'm going to live with her. I'd feel more secure than I do with Angela. What wears me out is that she's impossible to domesticate. There's a false balance of contrary forces. She's afraid—with good reason—of living moment to moment, crippled in spirit. What can I do if she's anarchical?

Except imitate her since she's stronger than I: I am the product of a thought, she is not a product: she is all herself. She shattered my system. She's my ancestor and such my pre-history that she manages to be inhuman, though she writes with false order.

Angela is my aphrodisiac.

Angela doesn't seem to me to have subtleties. She scandalizes me a bit. Because she's freer than I.

Our extreme misery.

Wanting to understand is one of the worst things that could happen to me. But through Angela's innocence I'm learning not to know all by myself.

I'm exhausted by Angela. And especially by me. I need to be alone from myself, so much so that I don't even rely on God. And so I'll leave a page blank or the rest of the book—I'll come back when I can.

I'M BACK. BECAUSE THE PUNGENCY OF ANGELA PRALINI called me. Before her—as before a "masterpiece"—I feel an almost intolerable tightening in the chest, a desire to flee the emotion. That's what I feel with Fellini's movies.

What our imagination creates resembles the process God has for creating.

ANGELA: I take refuge in madness because the boring middle ground of the state of ordinary things is no longer left for me. I want to see new things—and I'll only manage to do that if I lose my fear of madness.

Life is little by little. Today I take half a step, the day after tomorrow I'll take another half-step. Such impatience. I want to swallow life down in a single gulp and then maybe something like dying. But my own blood is slow.

I want to show myself the dirtiest and lowest part of me— and only then can I forgive myself. I want to be forgiven for being so full of sensuality that it is an animal cry inside me, a taste of the harsh voice of the wolf desiring its prey, me! I who aspire to the great disorder of vile desires and the darkness that possesses me in the apocalyptic orgasm of my existence. My existence is the victim of a fatality. That is: I am, oh poor me human and weak and needy and begging. I want your smile, I want your velvet caress, I want the body-to-body struggle, both so intimate, so gullible lost children.

I cry out for absolution! Oh mighty God, forgive me my life of errors and the worst habits of feeling, forgive me for existing in the pleasure so luxuriant and sensual of the absorption of the miasmas of the body-to-body. I want an abyss for you and to receive you like a queen of Sheba. Are my desires base? poor me, for I have an unhappy and unsatisfied body. Oh God of the desperate, find me, you have the power to distinguish my small noble part that barely glitters amidst the gravel, find me! Now! Right away! Ah … Ah … Ah … you found me … How my soul flies, liberated just a moment ago by the encounter with myself! God FOUND me. HALLELUJAH! Hallelujah! And I found God in my deepest unconsciousness, in the sort of coma in which I live I managed to stammer the vision of the God—in myself! I, also chosen by divine pity. What glory. Ah, but what glory.

And death no longer has power over me because I AM NO LONGER AFRAID! I swim and sparkle in states of vibrating divine fruition. Now I understand: I used to try to open a path in the darkness, knowing only how to beg. But only when I became naked did the doors of heaven and perception open wide to let me pass. I who am such a spark. And so I join myself to You and punish myself no longer. I bubble so nice and calm, poor me. This is how it happened: when I saw that I could no longer bear the weight of myself, I went to bed and all coiled up as much as possible in the fetal position, this: reduced to zero, having therefore to surrender to whatever came to me, since I no longer knew the answer to what I was asking, I burning with a kind of inner fever. Then—having to surrender myself to the Nothing—the miracle happened: I could taste like food in my mouth the flavor of Everything. This flavor spread like light and the sensation of taste throughout my entire body, and I surrendered to God, with the delirium of a soul drinking water.

Ah, how wide is eternity. For that is what I saw: the serene wideness of eternity, the taste of the eternal. Then the body once all weak and trembling found the vigor of a newborn in its first splastic cry in the world of light. And all of me became strong and roused, like a haughty stalk of blond wheat. Thus, standing like the stalk of wheat because that's how it was, with natural nobility, I could face the grandeur of the God. Standing like a stalk of wheat, I burst into You and freed myself from having a distinct soul. I was the general soul of the world. I was no longer alone: I had found myself in the intimate and dazzling company of God. Whiteness. Infinite transparency. And my body radiated in circles of light. Of the light that receives me. And I, naked as a newborn, returned to God. And this return of the prodigal son that I was anointed me all over, anointed the fragile and strong stalk of wheat that I was. And God was the detector of lost souls. And I who once couldn't stand the sensation of the abundance of myself, thinking fearfully that this encounter was too grandiose and would annihilate me. Poor me: I addressed myself like a slave adorned with garlands to please myself as a slave—and discovered the simplicity and the nudity of a queen, who, because she has everything, needs nothing more. Bless me, God: I extend to You a mouth lacerated by the fever of a long thirst, I extend to You my four paws torn and bleeding from trying to cling to You. Come and fill me completely with Your great gentle light, Amen, I owner of nothing, at last, warmed at last by the breath of an infantile sleep, by the rosy health of the soul, which emanates from me to myself and ennobles my way of existing, I, holy vestal, drugged by the essence of eternity, I protected by the luck of extreme penury that, because I could no longer stand it, becomes richness. I no longer need to ask: God gives. I who breathed in my own nourishing warm breath like a child tucked under sheets and sheltered from fear. Something touched my shoulder and called me and I didn't recognize that it was God and I was afraid of the great solitude and the great silence that open in the soul when it is going to receive them. I was afraid of my own simple grandeur of a human person. I already had and experienced a bit of all kinds of tortured baseness and human ambitions—I am now almost free of the "sin" of the soul. I can finally give myself to the luxury of being free of myself and start to feel a certain Olympic peace.

Living makes me so nervous, so on the edge of. I take sedatives just because I'm alive: the sedative partially kills me and dulls the too-sharp steel of my blade of life. I stop shaking a bit. And reach a more contemplative stage.

AUTHOR: I think Angela's pinnacle, one of her climaxes, is this "mystical" instant. Only Angela will someday know if it was mystical or mystifying. Anyway, from what it seems, Angela connected to the existence of a reality of life to which it is uncommon to adhere because everyday life often kills transcendence. Reality is fragmentary. Only the reality of the ultrasonic and ultralight of the infinite is whole.

Perhaps the "union of Angela with Everything!" is no more than a great self-knowledge and a great acceptance.

ANGELA: I'm still half-submerged in mystical sensations. I drank a bit too much of that strong beverage, I got a little drunk. I'll say nothing about what happened to me, since, instead of mysticism, they might say it's mystification. At the same time that I was receiving the God, I was turned inside-out and also felt that besides God I myself had made belief blossom within me coming from my medieval darkness. And I, trembling flower.

I don't like to explain myself. I prefer the penumbra of not-knowing.

I live in provisional ecstasies. I live from the debris of a ship-wreck that the sea rejects upon the sand.

AUTHOR: Everything Angela doesn't understand she calls God. She worships the Unknown.

This ecstasy of illumination makes me suspicious. Is it spirit taking full possession of itself to its very fringes? Or is it a woman's body brought to the point of crisis and then of mirages outside of her but that represent a "throwing away" for a few instants of the notion of lowness and sin? freed of the body for finally having acknowledged it, she, free of the heavy burden of sensuality, accepted the idea of the intimate union of two bodies—free, the great abundance of the universe is loosed, universe that has its voice in the absolute and expansive silence, silence brought to us by the air we breathe.

This illumination of Angela's cannot make itself known in words. As the word "scent" tries to express poorly what we call "scent." There are no words pure in themselves. They always come mixed with: "I don't know what's happening to me."

I'm starting to think that Angela's state of grace might be real because the "illumination" happened right after a feeling of complete abandonment and suffering. Saint Catherine of Genoa said that "when God wishes to penetrate a soul, He first abandons it completely."

She reached an ecstasy upon losing the illusory multiplicity of worldly things and starting to feel everything as a whole. It is something that is nourished in the roots planted in the darkness of the soul and it rises until it reaches a "consciousness" that in fact is supernatural light and miracle.

What Angela does not know illuminates her and dominates her more than what she does know. It's not a knowledge that has consequences. In fact she doesn't even know what to do with what she knows.

ANGELA: Today I felt something absolutely terrible. I felt that I am not understood by God.

AUTHOR: He who emphasizes the ritual of faith can lose the point of faith.

Sometimes those who don't believe are more likely to receive like a shining miracle the manna falling from nowhere. This "nowhere" is the air. And the air is what others call God. I call God as He wishes to be called. Like this: I open my mouth and as a means of calling Him let a sound escape me. This sound is simple. And it involves the vital breath. The sound limits itself to being only this: Ah …

Ah … the absolute and good and shrewd indifference … Ah … and it's toward this Ah that we as in a breath go with our Ah to meet Him.

It's a matter of the vital breath.

Meditation is an addiction, you acquire the taste.

And the result of meditation is Ah, which makes gods of

us. That's fine but now tell me what's the point of being Gods or Humans?

It seems to please us to be able to say Ah. So I end up shot through by the voice of God and here I say like one lightly exhaling: Ah ...

We were born to enjoy this Ah, could being be enough for me? I don't know. I don't know what I'm talking about.

The plant needs water, light-heat-soil-air to justify being, and could it be that the Ah justifies us?

There is someone waiting behind our left shoulder to touch us and to make us say Ah ...

When I say I love you, I am loving me in you.

I'm not relative I'm infinite that's why in each being I reflect myself in each being I encounter myself.

The most perfect thing that exists in the universe is the air. The air is the God accessible to us. When I speak of things I'm not reducing life to the material, rather I am humanizing the inert. All of this is as I once said, I play fair. I'm not hiding any cards. And if I have any style, let it come and turn up because I do not seek it.

Every birth presumes a rupture.

I was invited to watch a childbirth but I'm not strong enough to watch the dramatic birth of the dawn in the mountains when the sun is aflame.

Every birth is a cruelty. Things that wish to sleep should be left asleep.

My wickedness comes from the poor accommodation of my soul in my body. It is squeezed, it lacks inner space.

It's what didn't ever let itself be folded into four paws by the pain of existence, that pain which every once in a while we must obey in order to keep living our nice middle-class lives.

I ask God: why others? And He answers me: why you? to all

of our questions God responds with a greater question and that is how we broaden ourselves in spasms for a child within us to be born. But—but peace on earth and tranquil light in the air. God who is the nothing-everything sparkles in a gentle glow of an eternal present, let us therefore sleep until next week.

And I? Could it be I won't become my own character? Could it be I invent myself? All I know about myself is that I'm the product of a father and a mother. That's all I know about creation and life.

We want to penetrate the kingdom of God through sins because if not for sin there wouldn't be forgiveness and we wouldn't manage to reach Him.

I took refuge in madness because reason was not enough for me.

I wait for what's happening. This is my only future and past.

Comfort is an abundance.

One day the comfort in God and no matter how paltry it was we learn this from being in the warm shelter of our birth.

To be useless is freedom. To have meaning would belittle us, we are gratuitously just for the pleasure of being.

And from the future we will consciously wait for the lack of meaning, a freedom in speaking, in feeling Ah …

Happiness is nothing more than feeling an Ah with relief, then let us raise our glasses and modestly toast an Ah to God.

Though it's hard for me to finish it hurts so much to say goodbye doesn't it? Well because in me it hurts Ah.

Why God?

Why not sit smoking and dying of hunger Ah it's because you want to be able to say Ah.

Do we exist simply to be relieved?

I pay attention only to pay attention: deep down I don't want to know.

I don't want anything.

God is abstract. That is our tragedy.

I am like the cicadas that explode from so much singing. When shall I explode? What do I sing? Do I sing the splendor of dying? Do I sing of my love that is so alive that it convulses? Do I sing the sorcery in the air? Do I sing the molecules of the air?

I'm frightened by my own power which however is limboed: could I kill myself in my desperation for despair? No. I refuse to kill myself. I want to live until I become an old and meditative being, comatose from a deep even indescribable and unreachable lucidity of the senile semi-coma. This senile semicoma resembles a numb almost-sleep of the upper layers of consciousness. In that state—I imagine based on the gazes I have seen in the gray, immobile old—in that state one can respond to questions and even conversations: the ultimate aims of the living man are easy to execute.

What's difficult and ultimately attainable is the half-unconscious and present lethargy—without past or future: like for a morphine addict. It's a state of unavoidable truth without words. This state is milky and bluish with flickering ruby-red splinterings.

I write to you so that beyond the intimate surface on which we live you might come to know my prolonged howl of a wolf in the mountains.

I distilled myself entirely: I'm clean like rainwater.

Quint-essence.

Transfiguration.

Let the author beware of popularity, otherwise he will be defeated by success. There is a time when you must take a picture of yourself. Hunger is always the same as the first hunger. The need renews itself empty and entire.

AUTHOR: When something happens I don't make the most of it. And then an illogical longing comes. But that's because the present time, like the light of a star, only later does it reach me in light years. While it's happening I can't make out what's going on. It seems to me that I am only sensitive and alert when remembering. I almost live, therefore, in the past because I can't recognize the type of richness of the present moment.

The forgetting of things is my escape valve. I forget a lot out of necessity. I'm even trying and succeeding in forgetting me, me minutes before, I forget my future. I'm naked.

ANGELA: When I ask myself if the future worries me, I reply astonished or fake: the future? but what future? the future doesn't exit. Am I complicated? No, I am simple as Bach!

I fear the instant which is always unique. Today, walking into the house, I let out a profound sigh as though arriving from a long and difficult journey. Disappeared people. Where are they now? When someone finds out call Rádio Tupi. Where is the disappeared Francisco Paulo Mendes? Is he dead? He abandoned me, he thought I was really important … And the walls of China? Before I see Christ, I want to see them. I want a ten-year guarantee. I'm afraid of having a tragic end. I'm hungry. And so I eat three petals of a yellow rose.

Ah, the intimate life I have with myself isn't enough for me because bats and vampires cry out my name: Angela! Angela! Angela! And I cross measureless spaces to reach the era in which I live, I who came from afar. There are secret things that I know how to do. For example: remain seated feeling Time. Am I in the present? Or am I in the past? And what if I were in the future? How glorious. Or am I the fragment of a thing, therefore without time. The meaning of time elapsing is missing plot and suspense and mystery and climax.

I remember the future. Harmony is foreseeing an instant-now the next musical phrase. The train of darkness connects commerce to commerce. Conclave and sponsorship. Oh! the wonder of mornings. I'll live until Saturday. And I won't be run over. How nice. The world in focus. Does next year exist? State of emergency?

AUTHOR: I am the prophet of yesterday.
The joy of life is.

ANGELA: Two-twenty a.m. isn't a time for anything especially on Saturday.

I shiver thinking in parentheses, oh my God, careful: I'm going to speak of the year 3000—help! And the year 40,000? I'm scared.

In the year 40,000 I'm so dead. Even more than you. Careful, be very careful, sir. Help, oh inclement blue sky. I said as calmly as I could: please-help-me. It's getting dark. And I without food or drink. I got hysterical, sorry. Am I by chance inside out? No, God save me. I want to be right-side out, ok? But it's so hard.

Author: You—I say to anyone—you're to blame for the ants that will gnaw my mouth ruined by the mechanism of life. Angela doesn't die death because she's already dying in life: that's how she escapes a fateful end by having a sample of total death in her day-to-day life.

And suddenly—suddenly! a demonic and rebellious avalanche gushes inside me: because I wonder if it's worth it for Angela to die. Do I kill her? does she kill herself? I pull back my reins though the horse complains. Because I just thought better of it. And I'll only figure it out after Angela takes a position regarding death.

Life is so raw and naked that a living dog is worth more than a dead man. I'm so shaken by this stupid discovery that I light a candle in memory of that buried man. He was so perfect that he died.

I always wanted to reach a state of peace and non-struggle. I thought that was the ideal state. But it so happens that—that am I really me without my struggle? No, I don't know how to have peace.

My question is the size of the Universe. And the only response that fills in my question is the Universe itself.

But something scares me: that if I search I won't find.

I discovered a power: the power of being in a locked room: I imprison myself and become concrete. Though I continue being an abstraction. It's not contradictory to make oneself concrete and abstract: I become concrete on a level that is not that on which the world is planned. I obtain myself in the concretely possible that exists within abstraction.

I want to justify death.

Could it be that, after we die, we sometimes wake up startled?

There is a mystery in a cup of water: watching the calm water I seem to read into it the substance of life. Like a fortune-teller before her sparkling crystal ball. This story still hasn't happened. It will happen in the future. The future is already with me and it won't make me out-of-date. Or will it?

I'm an insistent question but I don't hear an answer. No one's ever answered me. I try in vain to find the answer in Angela. I keep my ears open to hear it. As if my shouted question would give me more than the echo of the question. I know that all of life is always nearly a symbol. But my heart wouldn't understand. So shall I always miss that thing? Can you live without that thing? I hardly answer.

I feel an almost insufferable and indescribable beauty. Like a starry air, like the shapeless shape, like the not-being existing, like the splendid breathing of an animal. As long as I live I shall sometimes have the almost-not-a-sensation of what cannot be named. Between hidden and almost revealed. It's also a shimmering desperation and the pain gets confused with beauty and mixed with an apocalyptic joy.

I'd like to live exclusively from my foolish and fertile meditations in the contemplation of death and God. I'd like to dedicate myself to kissing children. Deliver me I beg you all, I no longer want to be myself, I know that I am no longer myself. I am you. I feel the need to risk my life. Only then is it worth living.

—Angela, my love, I fumbled in the darkness of words in order to find yours. And my hand returned with a word that dazzled me: scentillating. I don't know what it means or if what I discovered exists. Now in the early morning there's a clear and delicate silence and the small shadowy garden seems like that of a cloister. There's a light inaudible trepidation in the trees: this trepidation can be heard with the skin of the body. Angela, as I create you I taste blood in my mouth.

ANGELA: We die.

AUTHOR: Deep down she doesn't believe that we die.

ANGELA: When I'm really happy I suddenly think that we die.

AUTHOR: But she's more frightened of life than of death.

ANGELA: Why do I exist? and the answer is: hunger justifies me.

Ah, that's it, isn't it? Well, if that's how it is then I'll take revenge and live my life with brutality, without pity.

AUTHOR: Why do I exist? and the answer is: hunger justifies me.

I get happy when I feel hunger, as long as there's something to eat, of course. Just to have an immediate goal. When I feel hunger, I have a reason to live. Or I want my life to be justified by the intense desire to live. What sustains me is necessity. Necessity makes me create a future. Because desire is something primitive, serious and something that impels.

ANGELA: I taste like tears.

I'm accompanied by organ and also by a recorder. A spiral flute. And I am very tango too.

I'm out of tune, what can I do? I was born crooked.

And hungry.

I get the feeling that someone is living my life, that what happens has nothing to do with me, there's a mechanical spring in some part of me.

What I want is simply this: the impossible. To see God. I hear the noise of the wind in the leaves and answer: yes!

There are so many movements around me that I thought of them: death awaits me.

My purest movement is that of death.

AUTHOR: Angela already learned to accept her crises of fear: when they come she immobilizes herself with her eyes closed and tries to forget herself to the point of becoming an unfeeling nothing.

I never achieve total immersion. Ah the day I can completely let myself go—that's what I'm waiting for. Meanwhile, there's Angela impenetrable rock of granite that she is. Or an aerial fluid I can't manage to breathe. She's always tasting a new fruit with pleasure and without fear of its taste. But she's clever: she knows that the only things that are poisonous are what the birds won't eat. The new fruit is an apple hidden and transfigured so as not to frighten and not to leave paradise. That's how she tricks her God. In order not to die, Angela prefers not to exist. I'm creating something that can only die by being forgotten.

ANGELA: To be happy is a great responsibility. Few have the nerve. I have the nerve but with a bit of fear. A happy person is one who has accepted death. When I'm too happy, I feel a gagging anguish: I get scared.

I get scared easily. I'm afraid to be alive because whoever has life shall one day die. And the world violates me. The demanding instincts, the cruel soul, the crudeness of those who have no decency, the laws to obey, murder—it all makes me dizzy just as there are people who faint at the sight of blood: the medical student with a pale face and white lips about to dissect his first cadaver. It scares me when in a glance I see the bowels of other people's spirit. Or when unintentionally I fall deep into myself and see the interminable abyss of eternity, abyss through which I phantasmagoric communicate with God. I fear the natural law that we call God. The fear. Suicides often kill themselves because they are afraid of death. They can't stand the mounting tension of life and the wait for the worst to happen—and they kill themselves to be free of the threat.

We leave an Alpha for an Omega and destroy ourselves and work and play and … For what? We walk toward a vortex— *irremediably.*

Doing nothing might yet be the solution.

They'd confuse that with suicide but it's mere coincidence. Does it make sense to run so much after happiness, could it be enough to be happy? Could it be that being happy is a state of tolerance?

AUTHOR: I want for my body good clothes, the finest French food, money to travel, a lover to love freely, a wife to take care of me. But all that while preserving my monkish soul. I know that it's possible. It's like knowing how to be alone in the middle of a crowd. It's like distinguishing your own voice that would almost get lost in a chorus unison of many voices: feeling the song in your throat and hearing yourself. I-must-must hear myself: because I have yet to tell myself certain things that are mysterious and sacred but with the taste of blood in my mouth. Things that are difficult to be fully lived for where is the true center of the pulp of the fruit for me to bite into? To finally shoot the arrow. But if I don't hit the target precisely I shall perish. Because of this fear I don't dare. My question is a matter of life and death. To die because of a word? If that word is filled completely with itself and a source of dreams—then it's worth dying for. But everything I do is out of fear of that word. It's out of fear that I'm split by a woman, the one I invented. At the same time I need nothing—plurified by naked simplicity. Now I'll let Angela go on talking about whatever she wants—so that meanwhile I can retire to my silence. Happy silence. I am a happy man because I was born. And because I know how to hold my tongue. To hold your tongue is to be born again.

ANGELA: I no longer know how things understand each other. Everything seems crazy. Today I took a taxi and my Christ-like mien made the driver of another taxi look back at me terrified four times. Oh human face that should be mine and is yours. I'm still alive though close to death.

AUTHOR: Note: I want to see if I won't forget to give Angela a face.

ANGELA: Sometimes I put myself in a situation of seeing just before really seeing. I foresee the next instant and musically my breathing accompanies the rhythm of time. I who feel before feeling. Harmony is sensing the next phrase, the next sound, the next vision.

AUTHOR: Death is beyond human measure. That's why I find it strange. I have no knowledge of its mute language. Or does it have a language possible for me to understand? It sometimes seems to me that death is not a fact it's a sensation that must already be with me. But I still haven't reached it.

ANGELA: After I've lived will I know I lived. When it's happening living escapes me. I am a memory of myself. Only after "dying" do I see that I lived. I flee from myself. Sometimes I hurry to finish some intimate episode of life, in order to capture it in memories, and, more than having lived, to live. A living that already was. Swallowed by me and now part of my blood.

AUTHOR: I'm filled with recollections and everything that is already the past has a touch of aching melancholy.

What do I do with so many memories—but die at last.

ANGELA: My aunt Sinhá died a happy death. She laughed at the moment she died. You might say she died from laughing. She simply dribbled around death: she didn't die at all. She just passed on to something else forever. She was lucid: like a lit chandelier, like organ music.

I feel that at this exact moment someone is dying. It disturbs me, that final breath, and in Ireland a strong redheaded boy is born. It's as though they were notifying me. To that robust child I say good morning.

AUTHOR: When we write or paint or sing we break a law. I don't know if it's the law of the silence that must be kept before sacrosanct and diabolical things. I don't know if that's the law that is broken.

But if I speak it's because I no longer have the strength to remain silent about what we know and what we should keep secret. But when that silent and magical thing swells too much we disrespect the law and shout. It's not a sad cry it's not a cry of hallelujah either. I've already said this in my book calling that cry "it." Could it be that I already died and didn't notice? Could it be that I already no longer exist?

I feel there's a finger pointing at me and making me live on the edge of death. Whose finger?

ANGELA: Yes. A bloody finger points at me. I shiver. Could it be the finger of death? I who survive myself, I queen of Pharaoh. But what I really like is a soccer tournament. Will I be alive during the next world cup? I hope not, my God, death calls out to me, so attractive and lovely. Oh death why don't you answer? I call you every day. I was made to die.

The ecstasy of cold champagne. The scientific ecstasy.

As for me, I'm just not up to the present: it's a bit beyond me. One could say of me: "she doesn't know how to take advantage." God said to me: come. And I went frozen all over. The ecstasy of the apocalypse.

But I might never die. I might be eternal and you too, my love. Will I be eternal after my death? Or am I only instantaneous?

I am essentially a contradiction.

The serene abstract graphic mark.

Banality as a theme.

Oh how I aspired to a languid life.

Twisted tree: witchcraft.

I feel an absolute anguish as if my arms were opened wide to the heavens in a receiving gesture and my lips half-open the better to inhale—as if I longed for the beyond. Beyond me. I surpass my boundaries and enter the air: the air is my space. Chaos had happened before and from that chaos emerged the spectacle.

I deserve a medal for living each day and each night three hundred and sixty-five days tortured by time. Only death settles it.

My God, give me the courage to live three hundred and sixty-five days and nights, all devoid of Thy presence. Give me the courage to consider that void an abundance. Make me Thy humble lover, entwined with Thee in ecstasy. Let me speak to this trembling void and receive in reply the maternal love that nourishes and cradles. Give me courage to love Thee, without hating Thy offenses to my soul and to my body. Let my solitude not destroy me. Let my solitude keep me company. Give me the courage to face myself. Let me know how to be left with the nothing and feel nonetheless as if I were filled with everything. Receive in thy arms my sin of thinking.

I live breathing my last.

Oh get out while you can because at all times the time has come. Every moment is get-out-while-you-can.

No one rests in the dentist's chair.

AUTHOR: What mischievous spirits are interfering with Angela's mental telephone line? because mentioning the dentist is something trivial that only a woman could come up with. Angela is capricious.

ANGELA: It's all rotten. I feel it in the air and in the people frightened and starving huddled in a crowd. But I believe that in the depths of rottenness there exists—green sparkling redeeming and promised-land—in the depths of the dark rottenness there shines clear and captivating the Great Emerald. The Great Pleasure. But why this desire and hunger for pleasure? Because pleasure is the height of the truthfulness of a being. It's the only struggle against death.

As for me, I discovered Death.

But how?! to die without having understood?? But that's terrifying! It's unworthy of the human being not to be able to understand anything of life. Yes. But mysteriously we go through the rituals of life. I give my life in homage to whom or what. I want to dedicate it, like when you dedicate a book. God doesn't kill anyone. It's the person who dies.

Even if someone. Defend my goal, God. I'm imprisoned for fifteen minutes. What delicious madness to write 13 as a number and not in words. I'll wait for you in the other world. First, though, I kiss my father and my mother. I shall be an infant rolling in space. Whose satellite? What a chill I suddenly felt when I said I was no one's satellite.

I'm serious as hunger. I'm terrified. It's dawning. I'm dawning. I'm the chord of a harp. Goal.

I'm serious as hunger. I'm terrified. My heart is in mourning. But it's dawning. Our seeds sprout. I'm dawning. I'm not a judge, no sir. I'm a sweet viola. Better than Carl Orff is silence. Goal.

What separates me from the world is my future death. Death will be my greatest individual achievement: a person undresses herself of herself to die alone of herself. Death is a biblical demeanor. And it has no discursive history: it is an instant. To die once and for all. The stopping of the heart takes no time. It's the tiniest fraction of a second.

AUTHOR: Angela's life is continuously at risk. Because I don't always have the strength to face her and her challenge. And, dealing with her, dealing with myself, I almost give in to the law of easiness. I force myself not to recount the events of Angela's life. But I'd fall into the descriptive and the discursive and that would cause me tedium and downfall.

Angela not only lives without explanation but also acts inexplicably meanwhile I keep looking at the almost always immortality of things. A stone seen as stone, that's when it becomes stone with its relative eternity. Angela thinks there's life after death but she's unequipped to understand what kind of strange inaugural life follows with an inimitable simplicity that life after death. Except life isn't the life we think we have and death has another name. There are those who know this because they saw in a glance their own ignorance of what is life and death. Those people live in a state of troubled curiosity while others, thinking that LIFE is their life and death is the end. And they will never be able to divine another truth. Without getting into the theory of antimatter in physics, everything has a front and a back, everything has yes and has no, light and darkness, flesh and spirit, will we end up in that antimatter after we die? How can we explain that every born body has spirit? The unexpected always happens for no one ever put a soul into the life that is born.

It's time for consummation.

Living is my code and my enigma. And when I die I shall be for others a code and an enigma.

Precipices.

I didn't know that danger is what makes life precious.

Death is the constant danger of life.

Angela's advantage over me is that she is non-spatial, while I occupy a place and even after death I shall continue to occupy the earth.

ANGELA: The future calls me furiously—that is where I'm going. Disaster? Who knows. When I think that one day I shall die I double over in laughter. Life is a joke. But everyone knows my true destination.

I didn't learn it but I know it.

While I write the irreversible minutes drip. It's Time passing.

I'm thinking out loud. Who hears me? I look at the person's face and see: she's going to die.

Last night I had a dream within a dream. I dreamed that I was calmly watching actors working on a stage. And through a door that was not locked men came in with machine guns and killed all the actors. I began to cry: I didn't want them to be dead. So the actors got up off the ground and said: we aren't dead in real life, just as actors, the massacre was part of the show. Then I dreamed such a good dream: I dreamed this: in life we are actors in an absurd play written by an absurd God. We are all participants in this theater: in truth we never shall die when death happens. We only die as actors. Could that be eternity?

Who knows, I only know I like diamonds and jade.

Don't think that I'm writing here my most intimate secret for there are secrets I never even tell myself. And it's not only the final secret that I am not revealing: there are many little primary secrets that I allow to remain in enigma. I surrender to the sweet familiarity of eternity. But I don't know if I deserve it.

AUTHOR: At the same time she gives herself the luxury of being sphinxlike. She tells me nothing of her soul. She tells me nothing of her secret fears. I'm the one who must divine her and support her like a gentleman. But I can no longer stand it and one of these days I'll let out my cry of freedom or make her kill herself. What I desperately want is to initiate myself in the fleeting Angela who is always escaping me.

ANGELA: Yesterday the world expelled me from life. Today life was born. Wind, so much wind. What instability. Me muero.

I live in the future of the wind. Why does everything seem to say: leave it for next week? I'm here, here waiting. I'm alive right now and the rest can fuck off. And my dog who didn't do anything. He just is. I too am: is. I with my tattered flag.

There are old people who die in the spring, they can't stand the bursting of the earth.

I want an elegant death. As a matter of fact I already died and didn't hear about it. I am my unnerving ghost.

AUTHOR: I live you as if death had already separated us. So intense is my longing for you.

Does everything I think about exist? why is my imagination poor and I only think about realities, and if it doesn't exist, then why do I think it?

ANGELA: An anguish. I'd like to live everything at once and not to keep living bit by bit. But then Death would come.

When I die I won't know what to do with myself.

There must be a way not to die, it's just that I haven't discovered it. At least not to die in life: to die only after death.

The world's getting ever more dangerous for me. After dying, the perilous danger will cease. Breathing is something magical.

I want my end to be as inevitable as death: my end in life will be possessing. I am virginal.

I almost already know what it will be like after my death. The empty living room the dog about to die of longing. The stained-glass windows of my house. Everything empty and calm.

AUTHOR: If they ask me if there's life for the soul after death, I answer, mysteriously as I am well aware, why not the mystery, if the thing really is mysterious—I answer in a hesitant out-line: it exists but it's not for me to know how that soul will live. No one has yet discovered the state of things after death—because it's impossible to imagine how the God will behave, the same God who inexplicably for us makes a seed sprout. I don't know how the seed sprouts, I don't know why this blue sky, I don't know why this life of mine because all this happens in a way that my human mind cannot fathom. I live without a possible explanation. I who have no synonym.

Life, life covered by a veil of melancholy. Death: beacon that leads me the right way. I feel magnificent and solitary between life and death.

Everybody knows everything.

Humanity is becoming hard. The facts are becoming bruising.

The morning is a premature flower.

Morning of never again.

One's incommunicability with oneself is the great vortex of the nothing. If I don't find a way to speak to myself the word suffocates my throat sticking there like an unswallowed stone. I want to have access to myself whenever I want like someone opening the doors and going in. I don't want to be the victim of liberating chance. I want to have the key to the world myself and to transpose it like someone transposing himself from life into death and from death into life.

ANGELA: At the hour of my death—what do I do? Teach me how to die. I don't know how.

AUTHOR: I lost the Book of Angela, I don't know where I left her life.

ANGELA: A work of art? No, I want the prime thing. I want the stone that was not sculpted.

I cured myself of death. I never again died.

I see everything as if I had already died and was seeing everything from afar. Then there comes that sadness of a cobweb in an abandoned house. What distracts is frothy hatred. Dry and lashing hatred.

Thinking is so immaterial that it has no words. Never forget, when you have a pain, that pain will pass: never forget that, when you die, death will pass. One doesn't die eternally. It is just once, and it lasts an instant.

AUTHOR: I still haven't reached myself. Do Angela's rags make her reach herself? My absence from myself hurts me. There isn't a single act into which I throw all of myself. And the grandiosity of life is throwing oneself—throwing oneself even into death.

"I want to die" with you of love.

So a dreamer I smile: yes, I wanted to die of love with a with you.

I am looking for somebody whose life I can save. The only one who allows me to do that is Angela. And as I save her life, I save my own.

ANGELA: A place in the world is waiting for me to inhabit it.
I was made for no one to need me.

AUTHOR: Somewhere in the world someone is waiting for me.
My face seems to say: my life is not significant.
Only after you die shall I love you completely. I need all your

life for me to love it as if it were mine.

There's a way of looking that makes you shiver. The forgotten and Spartan obvious way: the strongest wins.

Angela is stronger than I. I die before she does.

Once there was a man who walked, walked and walked and stopped and drank cold water from a spring. Then he sat on a rock and rested his staff. That man was I. And God was at peace.

ANGELA: It's dawning: I hear the roosters.

I am dawning.

— The rest is the implicit tragedy of man — mine and yours? Is solidarity the only way? But "solidarity" I know looks like the word "solitude."

[*When his eyes withdraw from Angela*
and she gets smaller and disappears,
then the AUTHOR *says:*]

— As for me I'm also withdrawing from me. If the voice of God manifests itself in silence, I too silence myself. Farewell.

I pull back my gaze my camera and Angela starts getting small, small, smaller — until I lose sight of her.

And now I must interrupt myself because Angela interrupted life by going into the earth. But not the earth in which one is buried but the earth in which one is revived. With abundant rain in the forests and the whisper of the winds.

As for me, I am. Yes.
"I … I … no. I cannot end."
I think that …

Notes

This book, incomplete at Clarice Lispector's death in 1977, was organized by her friend Olga Borelli and published the following year. The author did not have the opportunity to revise the final manuscript for publication. Clarice Lispector's style, even in the books published in her lifetime, is so strange that it is very hard to tell what is an error and what is a deliberate choice. We have therefore elected to stay as close to the original as possible.

In doing so, we are aware that we are not necessarily following Borelli's own process. Clarice wrote that "The I who appears in this book is not I." But Borelli understood that the connection was terribly real.

"She asks to die," Borelli said in her only known statement about the editing of the work. "I left out one sentence. I left it out to spare the family's feelings. I mean, the book was fragments, and one fragment touched me deeply, in which she says 'I asked God to give Angela a cancer that she can't get rid of.' Because Angela doesn't have the courage to kill herself. She needs to, because she says 'God doesn't kill anyone. It's the person who dies.' Clarice also said that everyone chooses the way they die."

On December 9, 1977, one day before her fifty-seventh birthday, Clarice Lispector died of ovarian cancer in Rio de Janeiro.

page 3 (epigraphs): "The absurd joy par excellence is creation." — This citation is actually taken from Albert Camus's essay "Absurd Creation." In the original text, this passage is followed by a quote by Nietzsche, which might explain the confusion.

p. 9: "But a journey with eyes covered thro' seas never before discovered ..." — The language here parodies the opening lines of the famous epic by Luís de Camões, *The Lusiads*.

p. 14: "The scent makes me sister to the sacred orgies of King Solomon and the Queen of Sheba." — The male figure of the "Author" describes himself here as "sister." We have preserved this interesting, perhaps revealing, moment of gender confusion.

p. 18: "Iansã" — In candomblé, the Afro-Brazilian religious belief system, Iansã is the goddess of winds.

p. 20: "immanescence" — In the original text, the word is "imanescença," a neologism possibly inspired by "immanence" and/or "essence."

p. 43: "I threw the stick ..." — This is an allusion to a well-known nursery rhyme. The complete first stanza would read: "I threw the stick at the cat-cat-cat but the cat-cat-cat didn't die-die-die."

p. 51: "I'm an Anonymous Society." — The original text uses "S.A.," which is the equivalent of "Inc." or "Incorporated," but in Portuguese the abbreviation stands for "Sociedade Anônima," or "Anonymous Society."

p. 58: "the God" — In the work of Clarice Lispector, God is often referred to with an article.

p. 91: "scentillating" — In the original text, the word is "faruscante," another neologism probably inspired by "fariscar," to scent or sniff, but the word is written as an adjective. It will appear again later in the text.

p. 102: "Georges Auric 'The Speech of the General.'" — The text refers here to "Le discours du general," composed by Francis Poulenc in the ballet "Les mariés de la tour Eiffel." The text misattributes this, though Auric also collaborated on the ballet.

p. 116: "Hudra" — This truck is actually called "Hydra."

p. 156: "I've already said this in my book calling that cry 'it.'" — This is a reference to *Água Viva*.